MONSTERS
MALEVOLENCE

MONSTERS
MALEVOLENCE

D.R. Mills

SEA OF INK PRESS

MONSTERS
MALEVOLENCE

Cover art: MiblArt
Interior book design: Enchanted Ink Publishing
Illustrations: Gabrielle Ragusi
Editing: A. P. Mobley at Sea of Ink Press

ISBN: 978-1-7358479-8-6 (Paperback)

SEA OF INK PRESS

For Grandma Betty

Thanks for everything

D.R. MILLS
PRESENTS . . .

MONSTERS

PROLOGUE

AN EARSPLITTING BEEPING NOISE shattered Owen Greyson's deep sleep. He knew that sound all too well.

As he rolled over and slapped the top of his alarm with a burly hand, he knocked over two empty beer bottles resting beside it. They clattered to the floor, but he paid them no mind, instead checking the time on his clock. *Nine thirty?* he thought, an aggravated sigh escaping his lips. This was the third time this week he'd slept through his first alarm and been woken up by his second. This was also the third time this week he was going to be late for work.

He ran a hand over his face, the rough surface of his five-o' clock shadow scratching his palm, and swung his legs out of bed. He didn't have time to shower, so a good dose of deodorant and body spray would have to get him through the morning. He was halfway done pulling on his pants when his cell phone rang. *Great, it's probably Griff wondering where I'm at.*

Grey looked around for his phone, but it wasn't in sight. He knelt down, almost falling because of his pants, and began sorting through the pile of clothes on the carpet. He dug through four pairs of jeans before he found his cell phone sticking out of the back pocket of a pair at the bottom of the pile. He slid the screen open and raised the device to his ear just before the call ended. "Yeah?"

"Rough night, Chief?" his deputy, Noah Griffin, asked on the other end of the call.

Grey glanced at the four empty beer bottles still sitting on his nightstand. "Something like that."

"Well, hurry up and get dressed. We got something."

The tone in Griff's voice made Grey curious. "What?"

"You remember the John Doe who survived that building coming down on top of him? The one who assaulted a nurse at the hospital before vanishing?"

"You mean the one earlier this week, or the one from yesterday?" Grey replied sarcastically.

"His truck is missing from our impound lot," Griff said hurriedly, ignoring Grey's sass.

Grey squeezed the bridge of his nose with his free hand. "Did you at least inventory the vehicle?"

"Not yet. That's what I was about to do."

"Great." Grey finished pulling up his pants. "Just gimme, like, fifteen to get ready and drive there."

"I'll start a fresh pot of coffee for ya," Griff promised, then ended the call with a *click*.

Grey shoved the phone into his pocket before zipping and buttoning his pants. He leaned down again, searching through the pile of clothes on the floor for a clean shirt. Several of the garments failed sniff tests, and he tossed them over his shoulder. Finally he found a tank top, and although it didn't smell the best, it was better than the rest. He pulled it on, hastened over to his closet, and pulled out a clean shirt to go over the tank top. *Guess I better add laundry to my list of things to do after work*, he thought.

He slid his arms through the shirt's sleeves and buttoned it up all the way, then grabbed his badge, gun belt, sheriff hat, and cowboy boots. Once he made sure he had everything, he hurried out of the bedroom.

He ran down the short hall into the kitchen, stopped at the fridge, and snagged a four-meat-and-cheese Hot Pocket from the freezer before tossing the snack into the microwave. As the appliance hummed behind him, he grabbed a bottle of his favorite bourbon from the cupboard and a flask from inside his jacket, which hung over a chair. He popped open the top of the flask and started refilling it.

Grey drank what was left in the bottle, set it aside, and stuffed the flask back into his jacket. Ten seconds before the Hot Pocket had finished cooking, he grabbed it out of the microwave, then bolted out the door, locked up his teal, one-story house, and took a big bite of his snack.

Hot pain seared his cheeks and tongue; he hadn't

waited long enough for the Hot Pocket to cool before starting in on it. It took all his self-control not to spit it out as he swore profanity after profanity. He opened his mouth wide and inhaled deeply, hoping the crisp morning air would ease his pain.

That seemed to work well enough for the time being, so Grey stepped down onto the short sidewalk leading out to his driveway and unlocked his truck via remote control. The vehicle was a dark green-and-brown two-door with a large bed and white stripes on the sides, and *Sheriff - Emerald County* stickered in black lettering over the markings.

Grey climbed into the driver's seat, cussing a few more times as he tossed his jacket aside, then started the truck, peeled off the curb, and drove away.

*T*HE TWILIGHT PEAK police station, like the rest of the town, was about as old-fashioned as you could get without being taken straight out of the Old West. The building was two floors high, with red and white bricked walls and a roof shaped like a pyramid. All the windows were four-paned, set in each corner of the building, and the hook-shaped lampposts outside had downward-facing light bulbs. It was beneath one of these lampposts that Griff stood as Grey pulled into his assigned parking spot and killed the engine.

Griff, who had only been with the station for five or six months now, was one of the better deputies Grey had had at his side in recent years. The kid was always professional, on time, and willing to go along with Grey when needed. He was also young, somewhere in his mid-twenties, and clean-shaven, his clothes spotless and wrinkle-free, his dark-brown hair cropped short. Griff nodded and smiled at Grey, one hand on his belt and the other clutching a to-go cup of freshly brewed coffee. All the while, Grey stuffed what was left of his Hot Pocket into his mouth, grabbed his jacket, and exited his truck. His tongue still stung a bit from earlier, but it wasn't so bad anymore.

"Pepperoni for breakfast today?" Griff asked.

Grey swallowed the final bite and wiped his mouth with his hand. "Four-meat," he answered.

"Whoa, Sheriff," Griff said, raising his eyebrows. "Mixing things up today, huh?" He handed the coffee to Grey, and they walked toward the station's front door.

"I ran out of pepperoni," Grey explained, and took a long drink of his coffee. As the warm, bitter liquid slid down his throat, he could already feel his body re-energizing like a battery plugged into several electrical outlets. It was nothing short of heavenly.

Griff smiled and shook his head as he opened the door for Grey. Grey stepped inside. "I stand corrected," Griff said with a chuckle, following close behind Grey.

"So, what do we know about John Doe and the missing truck so far?" Grey asked.

"Not much more than we did already. But we do have him on camera sneaking into the lot and getting his truck out."

"Good morning, Sheriff," a new voice called. Grey looked over to see Doris Habernackey sitting at her desk. She had worked here for years, and it was her job to take calls and pass them along to Grey. Her short curly hair was a mix of black and silver, and she'd always worn large glasses with thick lenses, giving her eyes a buggy, almost-alien appearance.

Grey gave her a quick wave. "Mornin', Doris."

"Mr. Ronson called again," she half-shouted at him as he continued walking with Griff.

"Oh, yeah? Was it the aliens again, or the nuclear, vampiric bears by Oak Grove?" Grey replied.

"He says he saw a shadow man in the woods," Doris yelled. Grey shook his head, laughing, and he and Griff passed through a doorway into the next room, a spotless area with varnished wooden walls and a white-tiled floor. Several other officers sat at desks here, writing out reports and typing away on computers.

"Mornin', everyone," Grey addressed the room, heading for his office. Once he reached his desk, he set his jacket and hat aside.

Griff followed Grey into the office. "Like I was saying before, we have him on camera stealing the truck," Griff started. "We've got the plates, and I sent out an APB before I called you."

"Then we just wait until somebody spots him and calls us," Grey responded.

Griff frowned. "We might need to do more than that."

"Why?"

Griff motioned at Grey's desktop computer. "You should watch the footage." There was a strange look in Griff's eyes. It wasn't a look Grey saw often, but he'd seen it enough to know this was something serious.

Grey pressed the power button, and a moment later his computer was alive and he was loading up the security camera footage from last night. "It happened sometime around three in the morning," Griff said as Grey began scrubbing the footage. "When we first found him, he was just some guy in the wrong place at the wrong time. But then he assaulted that nurse and left the hospital."

"Right," Grey mumbled.

"And now there's this." Griff pointed at the screen just as Grey found the moment their John Doe had entered the impound lot.

A man wearing a dark hat and trench coat appeared on one of the bottom-left cameras. He kept his head low, and his hat concealed most of his facial features. He seemed to effortlessly evade revealing angles from all the cameras as he sauntered into the security office that held the keys for confiscated vehicles.

It seemed to Grey that the John Doe had done what he was doing countless times, his movements so smooth and calculated it was as if he was moving entirely on muscle memory. He broke into the office without issue and headed inside. On another camera, he stopped and looked through the assortment of keys for about twelve seconds, then picked out his set and exited the office.

Back on the camera closest to the main gate, the man walked across the impound lot to his truck. However, once he reached his truck, he didn't get into the driver's seat. Instead, he popped open the bed of the vehicle and started searching through it. A few seconds passed before he slammed the truck bed shut, and although Grey couldn't see him very well, it seemed he'd become quite angry.

After that, the man trudged over to the left back seat door, opened it, and pulled something out from inside the truck. Despite the bad camera quality, Grey could see it was a massive hunting knife, the blade gleaming even in the night. The man sorted through a few other items–Grey couldn't tell what they were– before he reached into his coat pocket, pulled out a revolver of some kind, and tossed it into the back seat with his other things.

Finally, the man climbed into the driver's seat and started the truck. As he drove off the lot, all Grey could see were the vehicle's powerful headlights slicing through darkness.

Grey suddenly felt as though a heavy stone was weighing down his chest, and it grew difficult to breathe. He rested his chin in his palm and stared at the screen for a moment. "This guy is loaded up on weapons."

"And since we didn't get to inventory the truck, God only knows what else he has in there," Griff added.

It was apparent to Grey now what Griff was saying. There were far too many questions surrounding this guy to just sit around and wait for a call. There was no telling what the man's intentions were, but considering the concussion he'd given the nurse and all the weapons he had in his truck, Grey guessed they weren't good.

Still, something was itching at the back of Grey's mind. He knew this sensation all too well. It felt as if his brain needed to be scratched from inside his skull. It was a sense, or maybe a hunch. He wasn't quite sure, but he'd been sheriff long enough to know it wasn't a feeling he should ignore.

He slid the video time stamp back to the beginning and watched it again. Yes, there was a smoothness to the way this man moved–he was quick and didn't waste a single motion. In the dim light, and paired with the dark hat and trench coat, it was like he was using the night to camouflage himself.

"Something up, Grey?" Griff asked in a worried tone.

Grey paused the video and stood. "Head over to that fallen building and look around. See if he's been back there."

Griff offered a concerned look. "What about you?"

Grey finished his coffee and tossed the cup into the garbage under his desk. "I'm gonna go follow up with Ronson."

Griff's concerned expression morphed into that of confusion, but Grey didn't care to elaborate. He walked past the deputy and grabbed his hat and jacket, then left the room and started back down the hall toward Doris. *I hope I'm right about this…*

MALEVOLENCE

CHAPTER 1

"THIS SUCKS," WILLY SAID AS he walked alongside Ryan and Chyann, and Ryan turned to look at him. He seemed bored, moving forward with a dull expression on his face, his hands behind his head. As always, he wore his ripped jeans and gray hoodie.

"What does?" Ryan asked. "School?"

"What else?" Willy replied. "I'd rather be out kickin' ass and takin' names. School is super boring now."

"It's *normal*," Chyann corrected him. "And normal is what we need. I just got off my crutches. The last thing I want is to go looking for more trouble." Part of Ryan agreed with Chyann. Although she seemed to have overcome a lot of her fear, it was clear she still wasn't all-in on the idea of monster hunting like Willy was.

However, today a more pressing matter bothered Ryan. There was a chance Steve Helsing–the man hunting Boss–was still out there. Of course, Ryan figured the man had died back at the ruined construction site. But none of the local media outlets or even people around town had mentioned any casualties related to the toppled building. *If the authorities found his body*, Ryan thought, *wouldn't the news and paper have reported it?*

Boss also seemed to be holding on to the idea that Helsing wasn't dead, except he was more confident in the theory than Ryan.

"We might not have much of a say in whether we find more trouble, Chy," Ryan finally said. He looked over at his friends; they stared at him as if waiting for an explanation. "We didn't go looking for Woody," Ryan went on. "He kind of found us, and…" He trailed off. *Is now really the best time to bring this up?*

Chyann cocked her head. "And what?"

"Well… Steve Helsing, he–he might still be out there," Ryan finished.

Chyann rolled her eyes. "There's no way. And even if he *did* survive, he'd be paralyzed or incapacitated somehow."

"Yeah, man," Willy chimed in. "If he's not six feet deep, he's gonna be in the hospital forever."

"I'm less worried about Steve and more worried about us," Chyann added.

Willy scoffed. "Us? We took down Steve, a ghost, and an evil dummy. What's there to worry about?"

"*Us*, Will!" Chyann exclaimed. "We're seventeen,

in case you forgot. We can't just go around hunting monsters like it's a day at the office."

Ryan shrugged. "Why not?"

Chyann shifted her glare from Willy to Ryan. "What the hell do you mean 'why not'?"

"Think about it," Ryan continued. "We beat Woody and Adella, and considering Twilight Peak is supposedly attracting the supernatural, there could be more things like them on the way here."

"All the more reason to quit while we're ahead," Chyann countered. "We got lucky, and luck runs out eventually."

"So we're just supposed to let all the monsters and ghosts tear Twilight Peak apart?" Ryan asked. At this, Chyann angrily turned away from him. "What about Boss?" She didn't answer any of his questions.

Once the school came into view, Chyann quickened her pace, distancing herself from Ryan and Willy. "I'm not in the mood to talk about this right now." The icy tone in her voice was back, and Ryan knew he needed to drop the subject. But before he could even try to reply to her, she said, "I'll catch up with you guys later." And just like that Chyann was running far ahead of them, up the steps and into the building.

Ryan and Willy paused at the bottom of the stairs, countless students roaming and talking all around them, and Willy bumped Ryan's shoulder with his own. "She'll come around, man. She always does."

Ryan snorted. "Right…" He knew how Chyann got when she was upset with them like this. It didn't usually end in "she'll come around," either.

"Hey guys," the familiar voice of a girl called to them. Butterflies fluttered in Ryan's stomach, and he turned to see Sadie hurrying toward him. She wore her brown hair down, the curls flowing out behind her in the gentle morning breeze. Her crystalline-blue eyes and the silver shield necklace she always wore shimmered in the sunlight.

Sadie slowed to a stop beside Ryan, a gentle smile on her lips, and adjusted her light-green jacket underneath her backpack. Willy bumped Ryan's shoulder again, and Ryan realized his mouth was hanging open. He quickly snapped it shut.

"Enjoy your early hour with Mrs. Johnson?" Willy asked, his tone mischievous.

"I did, actually," Sadie responded. "She's very kind and patient with me."

Willy laughed. "Yeah, I bet she is."

Sadie looked around curiously. "Where's Chyann?"

"She's inside already," Ryan answered, hanging his head and starting up the stairs to the front entrance of Mountain's Point High School.

"Oh…" Sadie almost sounded sad, and Ryan had a feeling she sensed he was upset. The three of them fell silent as Ryan led them through the doors and into the main hall.

Once they reached the cafeteria, Ryan glanced at their usual table and saw it was deserted. *Of course Chy didn't save our table*, he thought. *Which means she's probably…* He walked toward the table, scanning the cafeteria, and after he sat down, he spotted Chyann at another table on the opposite side of the lunch room.

She was surrounded by three irritatingly familiar girls in their grade, and the four of them were laughing and talking away.

He pursed his lips in frustration. *I hate it when she does this.*

"Where the hell…" Willy didn't finish whatever he was about to say, and Ryan pointed over to where Chyann was located. Willy followed Ryan's finger, then rolled his eyes. "Oh, great," he said, slumping into his seat.

Sadie turned to look in Chyann's direction as well. "What?" she asked. "Who's Chyann sitting with?"

"The popular girls," Ryan told her.

Willy folded his arms over his chest. "The bitch squad." He rested his feet on the table and leaned back in his chair. "Why does she even hang around them?"

"Same reason as always," Ryan stated. "To get away from us."

"They seem nice enough," Sadie remarked.

Willy laughed. "Miranda? Nice? She's the meanest girl in this dump." Ryan cast Chyann one last glance, his eyes suddenly very tired. It was going to be a long day.

"ARE YOU SURE you're okay?" Sophia Shaw asked Chyann, concern lacing her tone. "That whole thing with Todd a couple weeks back was pretty intense."

Chyann turned to Sophia, who was sitting next to her. Sophia had always been an average-looking girl, her curly, bouncy brown hair a shade darker than Chyann's. She had large round-rimmed glasses, and she often wore a pink jacket with her name sewn into the sleeve. However, her eyes were by far her most striking feature: her left eye shone a bright blue, her right a warm hazel.

Chyann tucked a loose strand of hair behind her ear. "Yeah, I'm fine. Todd just gives me more dirty looks now instead of only focusing on Ryan and Willy."

"I can't believe you keep hanging around those drag-downs," Miranda Walker spat from across the table, holding her pocket mirror high as she applied a fresh layer of lip gloss. As the self-proclaimed "queen" of Mountain's Point High School, Miranda always had to look perfect, and today was no exception; she wore a yellow miniskirt and a black blouse, a matching bow tied around her wrist.

Miranda put her lip gloss away and adjusted her long blonde hair, then lowered her mirror and narrowed her eyes at Chyann. "That can't be good for your reputation," she continued. "If you weren't friends with us, everyone would probably hate you as much as they hate Ryan and Willy."

"Come on, Miranda," Sophia whined. "Can we spend five minutes around Chy without bashing her friends, please?" Chyann shifted uncomfortably in her seat. Sure, she was angry with Ryan and Willy, but that didn't mean she wanted to spend her morning trashing them.

Miranda turned sharply in Sophia's direction.

"Riddle me this. What else does Chy have going for her?"

"A lot, actually," Sophia retorted.

"Right here, guys," Chyann said, but the announcement fell on deaf ears.

Miranda threw her hands in the air. "So what's the deal then? Why don't guys fall at her feet?"

"Because those freaks ruin her reputation," Lisa Morris finally piped up. Lisa was the quietest member of the group, and as long as Chyann had known her, she'd stuck close to Miranda. She had on a blue coat and dark skinny jeans, her black hair styled into a banged bob that she'd maintained throughout the majority of high school.

Miranda nodded and pointed at Lisa, and Lisa rolled her eyes at Sophia, as if the answer to Miranda's question had been obvious. As usual, though, Lisa was only regurgitating whatever Miranda thought.

"Guys," Sophia said in exasperation.

Miranda sighed and leaned back in her seat. "Fine."

Sophia looked relieved. "Thank you."

"Let's talk about the new girl instead," Miranda suggested, giving Chyann a questioning gaze.

"You mean Sadie?" Chyann asked.

Miranda tilted her head. "Do you know any other new girls around here?"

Chyann crossed her arms. "What about her?"

Miranda looked over to where Ryan, Willy, and Sadie were sitting. "She seems pretty enough. What's she like?"

"She's nice," Chyann answered. "Why?"

Miranda smiled sweetly. "Just wondering."

Despite Miranda's words, Chyann suspected there was more to her wondering about Sadie. In Chyann's experience, nothing was ever so simple with Miranda. But, on the other hand, Chyann had no idea why Miranda *would* be wondering about Sadie in the first place.

Is she jealous? Chyann wondered. *Maybe looking to induct Sadie into the group?* Still, neither of those seemed quite right, and Chyann had a feeling this would irk her until she figured out what Miranda was thinking.

Before she could press the issue, the bell rang. She and her friends rose from their chairs and tossed their backpacks over their shoulders.

"Ready for Physics?" Sophia asked her.

"As ready as I'll ever be," Chyann responded with false enthusiasm as she and Sophia headed toward the main hall. Students herded around them, everyone scurrying to their classes, and Chyann couldn't help but recall her conversation with Ryan and Willy earlier.

It baffled her how much Ryan had already accepted the idea of hunting monsters. *Even just thinking about it right now is crazy*, she thought. *So why has he resigned himself to do it?* And then there was Willy. He, of course, wanted more of the excitement and danger supernatural creatures brought.

Didn't either of them value their own safety? What about hers? As for Boss… Maybe, if they worked together, they could find a way to fix that fiasco. There had to be a way to split Ryan and Boss up, right? But hunting monsters, keeping Twilight Peak safe from dangerous threats? It was too much. If they tried doing something so drastic, they were going to get seriously hurt–or worse. For crying out loud, they were still in high school! Battling the supernatural wasn't Chyann's job, and it wasn't Ryan's or Willy's, either.

"Heads up, Chy," Sophia whispered, snapping Chyann from her thoughts. Soon she spotted a familiar face ahead of her in the hall. Todd Hallow leaned against a locker, three of his friends standing around him. Chyann didn't know his friends' names, but she recognized them because they hung around Todd often.

Chyann's stomach churned as she and Sophia walked by the boys. All four fell silent, focusing on Chyann as she passed.

Todd's companions sneered and glared, but Todd remained expressionless. There was no anger on his face, no sadness, not even a hint of his usual smirk, and his normally somewhat-styled hair was disheveled, dark circles under his eyes.

Soon Chyann and Sophia were farther down the hall, away from the boys, and even though Chyann hadn't looked back, she could feel Todd's emotionless stare following her. Perhaps she was still a little shaken from her fight with him, or maybe just on edge because of the events of the past several weeks. At any rate, something about Todd was setting off alarm bells in her head, his lack of malevolence terrifying her more than Adella and Woody ever had.

CHAPTER 2

GARY RONSON WAS A STRANGE man, and the best way–or rather, the most accurate way–Grey could describe him was as the resident town kook. On average, Grey received a dozen calls from Ronson every week. The calls ranged from UFO sightings to ghosts in the sewers, and Grey's personal favorite: the "evil, demonic cartoon mouse."

Sure, Grey had been the sheriff of Twilight Peak long enough to know the town was weird. He'd seen his share of strange things while growing up here, and he'd only witnessed more odd occurrences once he'd stepped into law enforcement. But Ronson's reports were something else entirely. Whole leagues above anything Grey would call weird.

In short, the man was a laughingstock back at the

office, and Grey often heard his deputies cracking jokes at Ronson's expense. Despite it all, Grey sat in his truck, driving himself out to the man's residence.

For once, Ronson had reported something Grey had also witnessed, and Grey's thoughts shifted from Ronson to the security camera footage he'd watched earlier.

Grey recalled the effortless, smooth, almost-haunting movements of the man cloaked in the night. Maybe it was a long shot, but it struck Grey as more than coincidence that Ronson said he'd seen a "shadow man" in the woods around the same time this morning.

Pine trees and winding roads were all Grey could see as he drove. Ronson lived quite a ways out of town, almost on the other side of Mount Maddox. Finally, at the end of his forty-five minute drive, Grey spotted the gated path leading to Ronson's cabin.

He steered his truck to the side of the road, put it in park, and climbed out. A tall rusted ranch gate blocked off a path into the woods, the trail lined by miles upon miles of barbed wire posts that he knew circled a majority of the woods. It took minimal effort to unwrap the chain holding the gate shut, and then he pushed it open. Once the entrance was extended wide enough for him to drive through, he returned to his truck and continued his journey into the thick woods.

The farther he drove, the less he could see past the rows of trees. It wasn't his first time traveling this deeply into what most of the town called the "Witch's Woods," but it still made him nervous. *I hate it out here*, he thought. *I'd probably be crazy if I lived in these woods, too.*

It took another few minutes of driving before he arrived at the wide clearing Ronson's home was located in. The cabin seemed big enough for a family of four, but as far as Grey knew, Ronson had always lived out here by himself. Several trucks of different make, model, and color were parked all around the clearing. None of them looked very functional, though.

Grey pulled his vehicle up to the closest pickup, killed the engine, and settled into his seat, studying the cabin. *I'm really about to step into this nuthouse, huh?* The structure was fashioned from dark-oak logs. Three sizable bay windows occupied the front-right side of the home, and a wide, concrete-brick chimney rose stoutly from the top-left side. An eight-foot-high chain-link fence caged off the entrance in a way that reminded Grey of the military or some kind of security enclosure.

He let out an aggravated sigh before climbing out of his truck and approaching the front door. It had been years since Grey had last spoken to Ronson. It had been even longer since he'd seen the man face-to-face. All of Ronson's messages were filtered through Doris back at the station, and Grey only had a vague idea of what to expect inside.

Grey tugged on the gate handle, but it failed to budge, so he pulled on it harder to confirm it wasn't just stuck. When it still wouldn't open, a quick inspection revealed the reason. There was a bulky latch on the inside keeping it locked. Above that was a welded button pad on the fence pole, and sitting on top of the button pad was a metal plate with the words *ring for entry* engraved on the surface.

Grey groaned and pressed the button. An electronic *buzzzzzz* sounded until he lifted his finger again, and a moment later the gate unlatched and swung open. He proceeded toward the front door, and once he reached it, he pounded on it a couple of times with a closed fist. "Ronson, open up."

"Step back from the door," the voice of a man commanded from a speaker overhead. Grey looked up and quickly spied the device bolted into the wall next to a security camera with a blinking red light. He also recognized the voice on the other end. It sounded a little garbled because of the speaker, but there was no doubt it belonged to Ronson. *He sounds just as batshit as he did the last time I talked to him*, Grey thought.

Grey raised a hand at the camera. "Seriously?"

"Put your weapons into the drop box and show me your hands," Ronson ordered through the speaker.

Grey glanced down and found the drop box to the left of the front door. "I'm not putting my gun in there," he said.

"Then you're not coming in," Ronson replied matter-of-factly.

"Open the door," Grey growled.

"Drop your weapons in the box and show me your hands." Grey glared daggers into the camera. *This idiot is gonna be the death of me.*

Despite his reluctance, a moment's debate settled the decision. Grey opened the drop box, removed his sidearm from its holster, and placed the revolver inside, then released the drop box's handle and let it slide shut. Firearm surrendered, he raised his hands and stepped away from the door. A series of *click*s sounded behind it, and it swung open.

Ronson stood in the entrance wearing a tank top peppered with coffee stains, his worn jeans full of perforations. His short copper beard appeared as thick and curly as ever, and it matched the mop of hair on his head. A red cast covered his right arm, a leather patch hid his left eye, and to top it all off, he had a shotgun aimed directly at Grey.

"Good to see you again, Sheriff," Ronson said, his tone cold.

Grey nodded. "Gary. What's with the shotgun?"

Ronson shrugged. "I get a little paranoid."

"You don't say?" Grey gestured at their surroundings.

"This is fun, huh?" Ronson continued. "We're having barrels of fun already, but you didn't come here for fun, did you, Grey?"

"'Fraid not, no."

"Well then"–Ronson pumped the shotgun and tilted his head–"why are you here?"

It took copious amounts of concentration for Grey not to ball his fists in anger. It was as though every time Ronson talked, a fire deep inside of Grey was being stoked, and he was almost certain steam would soon be shooting from his ears. "Because you called me?"

"And?" Ronson said with a laugh. "I call you practically every other goddamn day, and you don't get back to me. What's changed?"

"What's changed is that I might have seen something you reported." He signaled to Ronson that he was going to reach into his pocket and, very slowly, retrieved his cell phone from his jeans. He tossed the device to Ronson. "Go to my videos. Watch the one I recorded today."

Ronson kept the shotgun trained on Grey but did as he was told. After speaking with Doris, Grey had recorded the security footage in his office, and that was the video he wanted Ronson to see. Ronson must have found it, because the man's eyes widened as he stared at Grey's phone.

"The shadow man…" Ronson whispered. He lowered the phone and looked at Grey.

"It's security footage from my impound lot that was caught early this morning," Grey explained. "The guy could be dangerous, and I need you to show me where you saw him."

At first Ronson didn't say anything, just stared at Grey with his hazel eye. He seemed to be debating his next move.

Finally, Ronson tossed the cell phone back to Grey and lowered the shotgun. "Wipe your feet," he grumbled as he turned and stepped inside. Grey pocketed his phone and followed.

The cabin's interior was a mess of papers, books, and various pieces of equipment. Ronson locked his shotgun into his wall-mounted gun rack beside the kitchen, which was connected to the living room. Grey walked into the living area, marveling at its massive size. It seemed to take up most of the cabin. He spied a spot in front of the bay windows that housed a table covered with loose sheets of paper and hardcover books with blank covers. Off to the side was a short hall that he imagined led to a bedroom and a bathroom.

"Can I offer you a drink, Sheriff?" Ronson asked, taking a seat in his recliner. It looked as if he spent most nights in the chair.

Grey shook his head. *Like I'd be stupid enough to drink anything this paranoid nut gave me.* He turned to look at more of the cabin's interior. Hundreds of papers were tacked to the closest wall, as were cutouts of names connected by yarn. Maps, newsletter headlines, and sticky notes had been pinned next to it all.

"What the hell *is* all this?" Grey exclaimed.

"If I'm on the right track," Ronson started, "the truth." Grey didn't question Ronson further. He didn't have the time or interest to humor the man on whatever "the truth" was.

He turned back to Ronson. "So, where did you see this guy? This 'shadow man'?"

Ronson shrugged. "Somewhere."

Grey clenched his jaw, digging his nails into his palms. Was Ronson *trying* to piss him off? "Are you saying that you forgot where it happened?" he asked.

"I might've," Ronson replied callously. "But maybe you can jog my memory."

"You want a damn finder's fee?"

Ronson smiled like this was a joke. "Please, I don't want money." He spat out that last word with disgust. "What I want is information, plain and simple."

Grey laughed. The action was forced, but it was between that and strangling Ronson, so it felt like the better option.

"Info for info," Ronson reiterated. "It's not everyday you follow up on my calls, so I want to take advantage of today while I can."

Grey threw his hands in the air. "Fine. What information do you want?"

"The casefile for Thomas Hutton." It caught Grey off guard how quickly Ronson responded. What confused him more was why exactly the man wanted information on Thomas Hutton, who'd been a scholar with a clean record. Occasionally, he'd even worked as a professor at the local community college. Grey had investigated the man's death just a week ago, and as far as he could tell, it was an open-and-shut suicide.

"Why that?" Grey asked.

"Because," Ronson answered simply. Grey waited a moment for an explanation, but apparently Ronson wanted to leave things at that.

Grey pinched the bridge of his nose and let out a frustrated sigh. "Fine, all right." Giving out casefiles wasn't something he was supposed to do, but he needed to find whoever this "shadow man" was. Besides, what was the harm in letting a three-page file on a simple suicide slip out? "You show me where you

27

saw that guy, and I will personally deliver you the Hutton casefile."

Ronson rose and stepped closer. For what seemed like whole minutes he stared at Grey silently, before holding out his cast-covered arm for a handshake. "You got yourself a deal, Sheriff." Grey shook his hand for finality on the subject. "Hope you got your hikin' boots on," Ronson continued, releasing Grey's hand. He walked past Grey toward his gun rack. "It's a bit of a walk there."

Grey took a deep breath. Now they were getting somewhere. But, as his anger began to subside, a new sensation replaced it. *Why do I have such a bad feeling about this?*

CHAPTER 3

STUDY HALL WAS SILENT ASIDE from the usual coughing or shuffling of feet, and Ryan sat alone at a desk in the back of the half-full room. As far as he knew, the majority of students at Twilight Peak didn't need an extra class to stay caught up on work. Normally, he didn't either, but ever since the death of his grandfather, he'd fallen behind in school. Counting Ryan, there were only about fifteen students in the class.

"Joshua, keep your mouth closed and your eyes on your work," Mrs. Johnson snapped from the front of the room. Ryan glanced up at the commotion. The teacher was glaring at a giggling boy in the front row. Once she addressed him, he shut up. The blanket of silence returned, and Mrs. Johnson resumed reading her book.

Ryan lowered his head, returning his attention to the journal on his desk, and scanned through another entry from his grandfather. The record recounted Grandpa Magnus's hunt and nearly unsuccessful kill of a deadly monster known as a Shimmer. There were several entries just like it in the previous pages of the notebook. *I could have lost him so much sooner than I did*, Ryan thought.

"*But you didn't,*" Boss chimed in from inside his head. "*And he fought evil like this for most of his life, you know.*"

"*Maybe Chy's right,*" Ryan thought at Boss. "*We're just kids, and we could have been killed more than once in the past few weeks. It's bound to happen sooner or later.*"

"*Perhaps,*" Boss responded. Ryan waited for him to say more, but he stayed quiet.

Ryan mulled over the idea of monster hunting, of following in his grandfather's footsteps. He didn't have to do this, right? Maybe if he went back to pretending monsters weren't real, he wouldn't have to see or hear about them. Maybe they would just stop existing.

It almost sounded plausible.

Except… it wasn't.

Ryan still knew there were evil beings out there. He still knew they were drawn to Twilight Peak. And he still knew if someone didn't stop them, innocent people would die.

He let out a long sigh. "*No… I can't just stick my head in the sand,*" he said to Boss. "*I should, but something deep down just won't let me.*"

"*Then we know what must be done,*" Boss replied.

Ryan closed Grandpa Magnus's journal and slid it into his backpack. "*We keep the town safe.*" He checked the clock to confirm study hall was about to end. "*Chy's in my next class. I'll try talking to her about this again. Hopefully I can get her to come around.*"

"*And if she doesn't?*"

"*Then… I don't know.*"

RYAN'S BENT AND slightly uneven chair sloped with even the slightest shift. It tilted back and forth as he wrote out a note for Chyann, who sat behind him as per their assigned seats.

Their teacher, Mr. Mardy, stood at the front of the class, explaining something about inertia and object mass. It was hard to say for sure since Ryan was more focused on getting this letter to Chyann finished. It wasn't out of the ordinary for them to pass notes, and hopefully she'd read it even though she was mad at him.

After several minutes of second-guessing his letter, Ryan scratched it out, settling on something other than words. He drew an olive branch, folded up the paper, and, when Mr. Mardy turned away, crossed his arms and slid the paper under his armpit. A few moments passed before the note was pulled from his fingers, and soon it was returned.

Ryan gingerly lifted the sheet and unfolded it. Chyann had added flames and a gas can to the picture, and she'd scribbled out the olive branch with black ink.

Ryan let out a frustrated breath. *Funny, Chy*, he thought. *Real funny.* He lifted his pencil and wrote, *Can we talk about this?* under the drawing, refolded it, and passed it back.

Chyann took the note. She handed it back to Ryan again, and he found she'd written *No* beneath his question.

Ryan contemplated what to say next. *We're going to have to at some point*, he wrote, and handed it to her.

Chyann seized the paper. He could hear her writing furiously behind him. *There's nothing to talk about*, was her response, and Ryan pursed his lips. Didn't she understand how serious this was? He picked up his pencil and formulated a reply.

There's a LOT to talk about, he wrote. *Think about all the innocent people who could die if we don't stop these threats. Think about Bobby. You didn't let Woody hurt him, so why would you let other monsters hurt anyone else?* He gave the note back to Chyann. It took a while, but eventually she accepted the paper.

It felt like forever before Ryan heard the sound of paper crumpling, and then Chyann shoved the ruined note into his hand. He hung his head in defeat.

"*It seems she's still upset,*" Boss said to him.

"*Gee, you think?*" He pulled the crushed paper ball apart to read her written response. *If you pass one more note to me, I'm moving seats.*

The words had been pressed so hard into the paper that some letters had ripped through it. He re-crumpled it and set it aside. *"Well, this is going great,"* he thought sarcastically at Boss.

"Really?" Boss asked with a hint of confusion. *"I thought that went rather poorly."*

Ryan put his face in his hands. Could today get any worse?

*L*EAVES *CRUNCHED* UNDER Grey's feet as he followed Ronson through the endless woods. The air was damp, the only sounds that of the men trekking down the path. It was almost too quiet.

Grey tilted his head back and scanned the trees overhead. Something felt off, but he couldn't for the life of him figure out what. Maybe he was just jittery.

Halcyon Forest–or the Witch's Woods, as the citizens of Twilight Peak called it–was a thick expanse of pine and oak trees surrounding Mount Maddox on all sides. Twilight Peak itself was nestled at the base of the mountain in an area where a good portion of the woods had been cut down by early settlers.

Ever since Grey was a kid, he'd hated Halcyon Forest. Something about the way the greenery tangled up and around everything, untamed and merciless, made him uneasy. Not only that, but ever since the "witch" who once lived out here had died, something was... different. The town changed. And the shift wasn't for better or worse; it was just change. The town's sparkle dulled.

Businesses closed, new ones opened. Some folks became recluses, some left entirely. Then new faces started moving in. Twilight Peak stopped being Twilight Peak, became any other mountain town. In fact, most people didn't even know the forest was called anything other than Witch's Woods. It was as if the evil fate that had befallen this place all those years ago had stained the entire countryside.

A sharp tug on Grey's sleeve snapped him out of his thoughts. He paused and turned around. Ronson stared at him, his lips turned down in a frown beneath his mustache. Grey hadn't realized it until now, but Ronson must have stopped and let Grey walk ahead of him.

Grey yanked free of the man's grasp. "What?"

Ronson said nothing. Instead, he pivoted and bent over, then grabbed a large stick from the ground, held it out like a cane, and pressed the tip into the earth in front of Grey's boots.

A loud metal *snap* sounded. The noise shattered the unnatural silence of the woods, and Grey couldn't help but jump. Pulse racing, he looked down to see a massive set of silver teeth had sprung up from the ground, splintering the branch Ronson had stuck into them.

"You're welcome," Ronson said as he tossed the remains of the stick aside and continued walking.

It took Grey a moment to steady his breathing and process what had just happened. Once he did–once he realized the gravity of the situation–he hastened after Ronson, nostrils flaring. "Was that a bear trap?"

"No," Ronson answered. "It was the cyborg-gophers from Yukanstanza." He shook his head. "Of course it was a bear trap."

"W-why?" was all Grey managed to choke out.

"It's in the name. *Bear. Trap.*"

"I know what a bear trap is! I mean why is there a bear trap all the way out here?"

"I put it there," Ronson said casually, and Grey didn't know how to reply. He was dumbstruck. Completely baffled. There weren't even coyotes in Twilight Peak, much less bears. In truth, there weren't many creatures besides rabbits and birds, and the occasional deer.

"What did you put it there for?" Grey cried. "And so help me God, if you say 'for bears,' I'll shoot you."

Ronson scoffed. "Of course it's not for bears, Sheriff. We don't have bears out here." Grey opened his mouth to respond, but Ronson cut him off. "We don't have *any* animals out here."

Grey furrowed his brow. "What do you mean?"

"Think about it. How often do you get reports about wild animals?"

Grey thought back to all the years he'd been Sheriff, then to his early days as a deputy.

He could name once, maybe twice when somebody had spotted a lone wolf or a small pack. There had also been a single instance when a deer caused a four-car crash outside of town.

He recalled animal attacks occurring here and there as well, but...

"Been a while, right?" Ronson interrupted Grey's

memories. "That's because animals don't like these woods anymore."

It was then that Grey realized something: why the forest was so strangely quiet. He focused on the trees once again, listening intently.

Silence.

There are no birds, he thought. And it was true. No chirping, no mating calls despite the fact that it was springtime. No movement save for branches swaying in the wind.

"You might find some cute little woodland critters closer to town," Ronson went on. "Where the people are. But not out here. Not this far away from Twilight Peak. Other things live in these woods now, Sheriff."

"What other things?" Grey asked.

Ronson didn't respond. He just moved along, rifle in hand.

Grey mulled over Ronson's words for a short while before letting them go. Ronson was crazy; Grey had to remind himself of that. The psycho was probably trying to get under his skin.

Still, as they continued their journey, Grey found it difficult not to humor Ronson's sentiments. Because crazy or not, Ronson was right about one thing.

There were no animals in these woods.

CHAPTER 4

NORMALLY, THE WALK HOME WAS Willy's favorite time of the day. At that point, school was over, and the rest of the evening could be reserved for fun and games.

Except today was different. Sadie had joined them, and she walked alongside Willy. Ryan and Chyann marched in front of them, the air ripe with tension ever since the four had left school.

As they neared their neighborhood, Willy leaned over to Sadie. "It's usually only this quiet when they're mad at each other."

"We're not mad at each other," Ryan said. "We're just not on the same page."

Chyann huffed. "Clearly."

Ryan turned to Chyann. "What do you want me to say?"

"Hmmm." Chyann tilted her head to the side. "Something along the lines of 'hunting monsters is a bad idea' and 'I'm sorry, Chy' would be nice."

"I can't just bury my head in the sand," Ryan argued. "And neither can you."

Chyann scoffed. "Watch me."

Willy quickened his pace and stepped between them. He hadn't meant to start a fight. "Guys, chill out. I was kiddin'. Sheesh."

"Why are you so against this?" Ryan asked, pausing in the middle of the sidewalk.

Chyann stopped a few paces ahead and turned around to look at Ryan. "Did you ever consider that maybe I'm being the rational one here? That maybe I don't want any of us to get hurt again?"

"Guys," Willy interjected.

Ryan shook his head. "No, you just don't want to end up like your sister."

Chyann crossed her arms, and Willy shoved Ryan back. "Dude," Willy started. "Seriously, st–"

"You got me," Chyann interrupted. "Mystery solved." Ryan didn't respond right away, probably because of the tone in her voice. It was a tone Willy knew meant Ryan better tread carefully.

Willy also knew how sensitive a subject Cassidy was to Chyann. Years ago, the Wakeman family had been ordinary, happy. But everything had changed when the elder Wakeman sister vanished. After that, the family fell apart. Chyann's father left his wife and remaining daughter, and Willy went from spending most nights with Chyann and her family to spending most nights with Chyann at Ryan's house.

"Maybe," Ryan began tentatively, "this is your chance to find out what really happened to Cassidy." Chyann grimaced, shaking her head. "If she got caught up in everything," he went on, "if she found out monsters are real, then maybe she worked with my grandpa at some point. Maybe he knew what happened to her."

"So Magnus just stood around all these years and lied not only to you, but to me, too?" Chyann cried.

"I don't know," Ryan said. "But he's at the center of all this. He had to have known something. There's dark secrets all over this town, and he defended it for years. But now he's gone, and–"

"That doesn't make monster hunting *your* responsibility!" Chyann shrieked.

Ryan shrugged. "Maybe, maybe not. But who's gonna step up if I don't? Nobody besides us seems to know the town even needs defending. Am I supposed to just let things go and wait for the day Twilight Peak finally goes to hell?"

"Twilight Peak was standing before Magnus died, and it hasn't fallen in the year he's been gone," Chyann spat. "So stop acting like his death was such a big deal!"

"All right, *enough*!" Willy shouted. His chest ached as if somebody had driven a knife through it, his palms stinging from how tightly he was clenching his fists. He shot Ryan and Chyann glares. All the while,

Sadie watched the fight with wide eyes. She covered her mouth with her hands.

Ryan looked down at his sneakers. His chin twitched slightly, a telltale sign he was fighting back tears.

As Chyann watched him, her angry expression softened a bit. "Ry," she began, her voice much gentler now. "You know I didn't– I would never–"

"You're right," Ryan cut her off. "It's stupid. The whole thing."

Chyann bit her lip. It appeared she was holding back tears of her own. "Ryan..."

"Don't worry about it anymore, okay?" Ryan continued. "I'll deal with it myself. You can go back to worrying about school, and homework, and your stuck-up friends. You fit in better with them, anyway." He hissed out those last few words before stomping off.

Willy's stomach dropped. *Great*, he thought. *I hate it when they get like this. Maybe, if I could just talk to Chy...* But before he could speak to her, she followed Ryan's lead and left, heading toward her house. Willy stood still as a statue as he watched them go.

Sadie stepped up next to Willy. "That was..." She trailed off.

Willy offered her a nod. He understood what she had meant to say. "Yeah."

"Have they ever fought like that before?" Sadie asked.

"Sometimes. It's always over somethin' stupid, though. Sorry you had to be here to see it."

Sadie had a far-off expression on her face. A few

seconds passed before she spoke again. "I have to hurry home to do my chores."

"Right."

She strode off ahead of him. "See you guys tomorrow, hopefully."

"Later." Willy hung his head. *Guess I'm going home…*

*C*HYANN DROPPED HER backpack on the floor and plopped down onto her couch. The fight she had walked away from mere minutes ago replayed over and over in her mind.

Why did I say that? she thought. *Why did I suggest Magnus's death isn't a big deal? That wasn't fair to Ryan.* However, it wasn't fair *of* Ryan to bring Cassidy's disappearance into their disagreement. So maybe Chyann had been somewhat justified in her counters.

She lifted the silver-and-black heart pendant hanging from her neck and gazed at it. Could Ryan be right? Had Cassidy worked with Magnus at some point? Had Magnus known what happened to Cassidy?

Chyann had wondered for years about what happened to her sister. Was the answer worth her life, though?

She dropped the pendant. *I should apologize*, she thought, then remembered the last few words Ryan said before stomping off. *He probably wouldn't even open the door for me right now, though.*

What else was there to do?

*R*YAN SLAMMED THE door shut behind him and stomped into his bedroom. "What the hell is her problem?" he shouted, hurling his backpack to the floor.

There was a soft flash of light, and Boss appeared over the left side of Ryan's face. "She's afraid," he said calmly.

Ryan threw his hands in the air. "So am I!"

"Take a deep breath, child. Stop yelling."

Ryan slid to the floor and sat against his bed, blinking back tears. "I can't do this on my own, man."

Boss nodded. "I doubt you will. It won't be long before the two of you make up."

"Yeah, right," Ryan choked out sarcastically.

"Do you know why my village lasted so long in those mountains?" Boss said. Ryan shrugged, and Boss continued. "Because we all worked together. If one of us fell, another was right behind to catch them."

Ryan sniffed. "What's your point?"

"You three remind me of home. Always supportive, always together, always 'riding shotgun.'" Ryan laughed, shaking his head, and Boss smiled a little. "Why don't we go back and speak with her?" he suggested.

"She won't wanna talk to me," Ryan replied in defeat. "Not after I dragged Cassidy into this."

Boss fell silent. His visible eye traced the air, and Ryan figured he was deciding how to reply. However, before he could say anything, three knocks sounded from the front door down the hall. "Perhaps I was right," Boss said. "Except it appears she has come to speak with you first."

Ryan rolled his eyes and climbed to his feet. "Shut up." He headed down the hallway and into the living room toward the entryway. Boss faded away as Ryan unlocked the dead bolt, turned the knob, and began to open the door.

Before Ryan could greet Chyann, the door flew inward. It struck him hard in the face with a *thunk*, and he stumbled backward onto his butt.

"Little pig, little pig," the familiar voice of a man called, and Ryan's blood froze in his veins. He knew that voice. He raised his head, saw Steve Helsing step into his entryway. Steve booted the door shut behind him and lifted his arms into a grand pose as though about to shout, *"Ta-da!"* A wicked smile turned up his cheeks. In a mocking tone, he said, "You're not supposed to let me *in*."

Ryan clambered backward. "H-Helsing!"

Steve lunged forward. His sneer grew wider as he took a small bow. "In the flesh."

Ryan continued crawling away. He wanted to stand, to run, but his legs wouldn't cooperate. "B-but how?"

Steve chuckled. "Pssh! Come on! It's gonna take a lot more than being crushed under a building to put me in the ground." He took another step toward Ryan. "But enough about me. Let's talk about you." He bent down, grabbed Ryan by the shirt, and lifted the boy up off the floor. "You're gonna pay for what you and your friends did to me."

Boss's voice exploded in Ryan's mind. *"Don't just stand there. Run!"*

Almost on instinct, Ryan swung a fist at Steve. The punch hit Steve square in the stomach, and the man groaned in pain, his grip loosening. Ryan tore himself from the man's grasp. He nearly fell over in the process, but he managed to maintain his balance and sprinted toward the kitchen.

"Get back here you little shit!" Steve howled from behind Ryan.

Ryan tore open the door to the garage and leapt inside, then slammed the door shut and locked it. On the other side, Steve rammed into the door, but it held firm. Half-dazed, pulse beating in his ears like a drum, Ryan grabbed the railing next to him to keep himself from falling over. As he did so, he caught a glimpse of Steve through the door's small window.

For a moment, Steve just glared through the glass. Then he punched it out and lowered his hand to search for the lock. Stomach clenching, Ryan spun around and hurdled down the short staircase leading farther into the garage.

Before Ryan even reached the bottom of the steps, he heard the door swing open, and Steve was after him again. *I can't go out the main garage door with Steve so close behind*, he thought. But there was another door across from the basement that led to the backyard.

Ryan bolted for the backyard door, but Steve clasped the hood of his jacket and yanked him back.

As he swiveled around, his cheek collided with Steve's fist. He struggled against Steve, scrambling to the side, and smashed into a cabinet. His body throbbing with new aches, his cheek pulsing with white-hot pain, he collapsed. Items from inside the cabinet spilled out and clattered to the floor around him. He groaned, his thoughts a haze, his vision blurry. It was as if his body was trying to catch up with what had just occurred.

"Make this easy on both of us, kid," Steve said, and Ryan's vision finally came back into focus. He spotted an old wooden cane resting on the floor before him, recognizing it as the one Grandpa Magnus had used years ago during his month-long recovery from a knee surgery.

Ryan snatched the cane, rolled over, and swung hard. The cane connected with Steve's leg. The man yelped, kneeling. Ryan batted it again, dealt a blow to Steve's head. Steve fell on his back with a grunt.

Ryan dropped the cane and leapt to his feet, but his balance was more off than ever. He stumbled over to the backyard door and yanked it open.

The afternoon sunlight sent waves of agony arcing through Ryan's skull, but he didn't have much farther to go. The gate was just ahead. He rushed across the sidewalk toward it.

Usually, a chain kept the gate shut, but all Ryan had to do was push against the fence to get enough room to slip through. He hit it hard with open palms and moved to scurry by.

To Ryan's surprise, the gate wouldn't give, and he nearly struck his head on it. He shoved it again, harder this time, but still it remained shut. He glanced down to find out why. To his horror, somebody had zip tied the bottom half of the gate.

If he couldn't go through the fence, he'd have to go over it. Ryan jumped, seized the metal wiring, and hauled himself up as quickly as he could.

As he swung a leg over the top of the fence, there was a sharp tug on his pants, and he was yanked back into his yard. He landed hard on his spine, breath catching in his throat.

Steve stepped into view, Grandpa Magnus's cane in hand. "Better luck next time, little pig." He raised the cane above his head. Brought it down.

The wood collided with Ryan's skull, and after that, he knew nothing.

CHAPTER 5

AND WHAT ABOUT YOUR SON, huh?" Willy's mother yelled from inside the small trailer home. He'd arrived at the house a few minutes ago, but he couldn't get in because his bedroom window was shut and locked. He sat on the steps of the front door, contemplating his next move.

"What about him?" Willy's father shouted back.

"He's always in detention! He's not learning anything."

"And you think that's my fault?"

Willy snorted, listening as they argued more. They'd be at this for hours. *No way in hell am I going in right now*, he thought.

"I'll tell you what I think," his mother said. "I think you're a terrible father."

"Shut your mouth! If there's anything wrong with the brat, it's your fault."

"How is it my fault?"

Willy stood and began walking away as his father screamed, "Does the phrase 'son of a bitch' ring any bells?"

Even when Willy reached the street, he could still hear his parents yelling, which meant the neighbors could hear them, too. He needed to get away, and fast. He didn't want to be here when the cops rolled up.

Maybe he could find somewhere else to sit and think. Then again, without his music, that didn't sound very appealing. Instead, perhaps he could bite the bullet and try regrouping with his friends. Well, one of them, anyway.

Stuffing his hands in his sweater pocket, Willy trudged up the long street. This neighborhood was large–so large it had a shady side, which was where he lived. Farther up the hill, however, were the nicer houses, which was where Ryan, Chyann, and Sadie resided.

Unfortunately, Willy's mother couldn't work due to some muscle disease, and his father couldn't hold down a steady job longer than a month or two. As a result, Willy's family had been stuck on the bad side of the neighborhood for years.

It only took about five minutes to walk to Ryan's place. *I'd better start there*, Willy thought, Ryan's harsh parting words to Chyann creeping up in the back of his mind. *This is more serious than any other fight they've had. What if they don't make up this time?*

He couldn't imagine the three of them not being friends. But what if this was the fight that ended everything?

He shook his head. *Quit thinkin' about it like that. They're not gonna stop bein' friends for nothin'.* With that thought, he trekked on. After all, they'd get past this.

They had to.

*H*OW MUCH FARTHER? Grey wondered, tramping after Ronson in the woods. *It's been almost an hour now.*

As if on cue, Ronson stopped and pointed at someplace up ahead. "Right there. That's where I saw the shadow man."

Grey reached Ronson's side and scanned the area before them. At first glance, it seemed like any other normal section of the forest. But as he looked closer...

Grey carefully stepped forward, watching the ground for more traps. *Hopefully there won't be any more surprises.*

The closer he got to the zone in question, the more outstanding details he found—most notably a set of tire tracks in the pressed-down grass. It seemed as though somebody had been parked there overnight. Furthermore, pieces of food wrappers and other bits of trash lay scattered around the tracks.

Grey recalled Doris mentioning a call they'd received this morning: a gas station clerk who'd reported a theft at his place of work. *Could this be the stolen stuff?*

At first, the call from the gas station clerk hadn't seemed too important to Grey, but now he was seeing a possible connection between the theft and his John Doe. In fact, the time of robbery was close to the time the man had stolen the truck out of the lot. After he got away, he must have hit the gas station for food, then stayed in the woods to rest. But where was he now?

Grey cupped his chin in his hand. "You're sure this is where you saw him?"

"As sure as hellfire," Ronson asserted.

It was hard to say for certain whether this was connected to Grey's missing fugitive, but it was as good a place to start as any. *What's he after? He could've booked it outta Twilight Peak once he got his truck back.*

For all we know, he's long gone by now. Except, something tells me that's not the case...

"What was that?" Ronson said suddenly.

Grey examined the surrounding trees. "What was what?"

Ronson stepped up next to Grey, rifle raised and ready to fire. "I saw something move behind that tree over there." He tilted his gun barrel toward a pine to the left.

Grey rested a hand on his holster and tentatively stepped forward to investigate, peeking behind the trunk from a safe distance. There was nothing on the other side of the tree, just dirt and grass and twigs, and Grey parted his lips to tell Ronson he was seeing things.

But before Grey could utter a word, he stopped.

Something shifted in his peripheral vision. He turned his head toward the movement and caught sight of someone in a dark hood watching him from behind a different tree. Grey jerked toward them, and they ducked for cover. "Hey!" he yelled.

The hooded figure dashed out from their hiding place and took off sprinting into the woods. Grey bolted after them. He wasn't sure whether Ronson was following, and, at the moment, he didn't really care. All that mattered right now was catching up to who-ever this was and getting some answers.

They wore a pitch-black cloak with a white image on the hood, but Grey hadn't gotten a good enough look at it to see what it represented. Their robe bil-lowed outward as they leapt over branches and rocks. For a moment, Grey wondered if this was his mystery man. However, that theory was proven wrong when he caught sight of the shape of the person's body; she had to be a woman.

Grey's chest began to burn. He pushed through the pain and quickened his pace. He had to catch up to her.

When he saw what waited for them at the end of the path ahead, he smiled. She was running directly for a cliff overlooking the river. There was nowhere else to go. Within a few seconds, the woman stopped at the drop-off and gazed down at the water. Grey slowed to a stop and drew his revolver. "Stop right where you are," he barked.

She glanced over the edge.

"Let me see your hands," Grey commanded.

The woman didn't obey. Instead, she turned around to face him, then leaned backward.

"I said let me see your hands!" Grey reiterated.

She kept her head down. All Grey could make out of her facial features were her lips and chin, and on the right side of her chin, she had an X-shaped scar. *Haven't I seen that somewhere before?* The rest of her face was hidden beneath her hood, which he could now see had a massive white eye printed on it.

Her lips curled into a cheap grin. She jumped backward.

"Stop!" Grey screamed. But he couldn't stop her. She fell off the ledge, slipping out of sight.

Grey lowered his revolver and dashed after her. There was a *splash,* and he peered over the edge of the cliff. The water rushed along, the woman nowhere to be seen.

Grey scanned the river's surface in search of her. She never reappeared.

C'MON, MAN. OPEN up already." Willy pounded on Ryan's front door for the fifth time in a row. *Ry's gotta be in there*, he thought. He stood for a while, waiting for Ryan to answer, but still Ryan didn't appear. "All right," Willy continued. "If you aren't gonna get your ass out here, I'm just gonna come in."

Willy turned the knob and pushed the door open, then stepped inside and locked up behind him. As he did so, he felt something cold and slimy on the wood. He raised his hand to see what it was. Mud was smeared on his palm and fingers.

That's weird. He looked down at the floor, finding muddy boot prints all over the white living room carpet. *Those are way too big to be Ryan's. What the hell?*

Willy searched the room for any other strange signs. "Ryan? You here?" He walked farther into the house, continuing his investigation.

Nothing seemed out of place, so why did he have this feeling in his chest? It was tight, almost like when he watched horror movies with his friends and the Final Girl was marching down a dark hallway, the killer waiting for her at the end of it.

It would have been easy to wave away the anxious feeling if Ryan just answered him. "Ryan!" He waited a second before following up with, "This is a really shitty time to be playing some kinda joke, dude." And he hoped that's all it was.

He headed down the hall toward Ryan's bedroom. The door was cracked open, light streaming out from what was no doubt Ryan's window. Willy poked his head through the door. *Ry's not here either... Where else could he have gone?* It wasn't unusual for Ryan to go on a walk to clear his head. That didn't explain the muddy footprints, though.

Willy doubled back to the living room and followed the prints into the kitchen, then toward the garage door.

When he laid his eyes on the door, his heart sank.

It was wide open, its little glass window smashed and broken, shards littering the floor. It was then that Willy knew for sure something bad had happened. "Ryan?" he shouted. Still no answer.

Screw this, he thought as he pulled out his cell phone from his pocket. The device wasn't as nice as his friends', but it got the job done. He flipped it open and dialed Chyann's number. *Come on, come on, come on…*

It rang four times before Chyann answered. "What?" she said. There were other voices in the background, but Willy couldn't understand them.

"Ryan's missing," he blurted. "I came to his place and he's not here and–"

"Are you sure he didn't just take a walk?" Chyann interrupted. "You know how he gets when he's mad."

Willy took a cautious step forward to inspect the garage door. Small drops of blood stained the still-attached pieces of glass. "Oh yeah? Does he usually break stuff?"

"I don't know. But today was…"

Willy sighed. "Different."

"Exactly." The voices in the background squealed and giggled, and Chyann shushed them. "Look, I gotta go," she went on. "I'm sure he's fine, okay? Just let him blow off steam and we'll try to work things out later."

"Chy–"

"Try calling him instead of me if you're that worried," Chyann suggested before hanging up. Willy lowered his phone and shut it. *She didn't even let me explain...* He sucked in a long breath, gingerly stepping over the broken glass and into the garage.

Several shards *crunch*ed beneath his sneakers as he went down the steps and looked around. Immediately he noticed another mess. There was a cabinet up against the wall, but its doors were open, its contents strewn about the floor. And it didn't look as though someone had been searching through the cabinet; it looked as though the cabinet's insides had fallen out somehow.

Not only that, but the door leading to the backyard was also wide open, sunlight pouring in from outside. Willy strode to the doorway and peered into the backyard.

The yard looked just as it always had, with a paved path leading to the back gate that Willy and Ryan had often snuck out through when they were younger. Wait, something *was* strange about this. On the path lay... a cane?

Willy hurried over to inspect the object. Sure enough, it was an old, dark-brown cane. That wasn't what troubled him, though. Blood was smeared all over the walking stick and on the pavement around it.

Willy's stomach twisted and turned, and he stumbled back, his thoughts racing with worst-case scenarios, his legs feeling like jelly. *I knew something was wrong, and Chy just blew me off!*

A thought struck him. Chyann had told him to call Ryan. He'd heard her clearly, but the idea hadn't registered until now. He snatched his cell from his pocket again and called Ryan. "Answer me, man. Please…"

A moment of silence passed before he heard it: Ryan's ringtone buzzing from the bushes next to the gate. Willy lowered his phone and fixed his eyes on the area the noise was coming from. He willed himself to move forward. Stepped toward the bushes.

What on earth was he about to find? Ryan's mangled corpse? More blood? He knelt down and peered under the greenery. Ryan's cell phone sat amongst the leaves. The ringing stopped.

Willy reached down and grabbed the device before turning it over to view the screen. Despite the cracks covering the device, he could still read the latest notification.

One missed call: Will.

CHAPTER 6

WILLY SPRINTED UP CHYANN'S driveway and onto her porch, then pounded his fists against her front door. Even through the loud music inside, she was sure to hear him knocking. When he'd found Ryan's phone, he'd tried calling her again, but she hadn't picked up.

After what felt like forever, someone unlocked and opened the door. However, Miranda stuck her head outside rather than Chyann. Willy had a feeling Miranda's unenthused expression matched his own. "False alarm on the pizza, girls," Miranda said. "It's just one of Chy's dogs." She smiled cruelly. "Must have broken his leash."

Willy mustered a confused expression. "Man, that's weird." He looked around, acting as if he was searching for something. "There's a clown here, but no circus." He turned back to Miranda, who glared daggers at him. "Now that we got that outta the way, move." He shoved past her and rushed inside.

Chyann sat on the couch in her living room with Sophia next to her. Lisa was lounging on an adjacent sofa. "Will?" Chyann said.

Willy dug into his pocket, retrieved Ryan's phone, and tossed the device to her. She caught it and stared down at it for several moments. Willy waited for her to look back up at him before he spoke. "Now do you believe me?"

Chyann stared at him in silence. Finally, she said, "Girls, excuse me for a few minutes." She rose from her seat and gestured for Willy to follow. Miranda and Lisa glared at him, but he didn't care enough to give them any sort of attention.

He followed Chyann upstairs and into her room. She closed the door behind them. "I found his phone outside," Willy said. "There's blood, broken glass, and muddy footprints. Something bad happened after he got home."

Chyann looked over Ryan's phone, her face expressionless. "Are you sure?"

Willy furrowed his brow. "What do you mean, am I sure?"

She crossed her arms. "If this is some joke to get me and Ryan to talk things out..."

"Why would I make this up?" Willy yelled, noticing her twitch as he raised his voice. "Are you serious? Do you really think I'd stoop that low?"

"Well, no, but–"

"This isn't some high-school drama, Chy. This is *us*."

She opened her mouth as though to reply, but ended up saying nothing. Silence hung heavy in the air as she fidgeted with Ryan's broken cell phone.

"You wanna be normal?" Willy finally exclaimed. "Well, too freakin' bad. Ryan stopped bein' normal when a weird cat-monster possessed him. I stopped bein' normal when I had to stand off with an angry ghost, and *you* stopped bein' normal when you kicked an evil doll off of Wellington's roof!"

"I'm scared!" Chyann suddenly shouted.

Willy shook his head. "You think I'm not? You think Ryan's not?" His response seemed to catch her off guard. Her expression softened.

She sucked in a long breath. Her hands twitched, and she hid them behind her back. "Why do you think we can do this?" she asked. "We're just teenagers, Will. Magnus was experienced and clearly knew what he was doing. We could go after something tomorrow and wind up dead, for all you know."

"If I die fighting a monster, then I die knowing I was trying to keep this town safe. I die knowing I didn't turn tail and run. I stood my ground and fought back." Chyann raised her eyebrows, confused. "And yeah, I might not know whether we're gonna die tomorrow, but here's something I *do* know," he continued. "Sadie, Jaci, Bobby–they're all alive because of us. Maybe that doesn't mean anything to you, but it means a hell of a lot to me."

Chyann hung her head, gazing down at Ryan's phone. Tears began to slip down her cheeks. She gripped the cell tight and held it to her chest. "I'll send the girls home." She looked up and met Willy's gaze, a familiar fire alight in her eyes. "Let's go find Ryan."

Willy nodded, and as he led the way out of her bedroom, the tension between them lifted. *Hold on, buddy*, he thought. *We're comin' to getcha.*

A DANK AND musty smell invaded Ryan's nostrils as he slowly woke up, part of him wishing he'd remained unconscious. His head felt as though it were lodged in a melon press, a quick, consistent pain throbbing in his skull.

He wanted to raise a hand to rub his closed, aching eyes, but his hands were stuck behind his back. Bracing himself for more pain, he slowly opened his eyes and waited for the world to come into focus. Wherever he was located appeared dim, but it wasn't so dark that he couldn't see.

He blinked a few times, soon able to pick out the details of his surroundings. He sat in a room, and aside from a staircase across from him, a wooden table pushed up against the wall to his right, and a large pair of double doors to his left, the place was empty.

He tried to move his arms again, but they refused to budge, so he turned his head and realized he was tied to the chair he was sitting in. Frantically glancing around, he searched for answers, anything to help him out of this. *How did I get here? What's going on?*

A flash of bright light in front of his face sent a shock wave through his body. When the blaze faded, he saw Boss hovering in his sight line. "Are you okay?" Boss asked.

"I... think so," Ryan answered. He hadn't realized it until he'd spoken, but his throat was dry. He tried moving his legs, but found they'd been bound to the chair as well. "Where are we?"

Boss looked around. "I'm not sure. Helsing put a bag over your head after he struck you."

The events of his attempted escape came back to Ryan at the mention of the madman's name. "Where is he?"

As if on cue, heavy footsteps sounded upstairs, and then a door *creak*ed open and shut.

Steve Helsing descended the wooden steps, a duffel bag slung across his back as he whistled a tune Ryan often heard on the radio. When he saw Ryan, he grinned. "Oh, good! You're awake." He sauntered over to the table and placed his bag on it. "I must have hit you harder than I thought."

Ryan shifted around more in an attempt to loosen the ropes. "There are people who're gonna notice I'm gone. They'll come looking for me."

Steve snorted. "Like your stupid friends? Yeah, I wouldn't count on them to rescue you." He threw open the bag's primary flap and began removing various containers, tools, and weapons from it. He inspected a few before placing all of them on the table. "Those two probably don't even realize you're gone. Not that they can track you here, anyway." Steve lifted a hunting knife and removed the blade from its sheath. He faced Ryan, turning the weapon over in his hands. "That means you better get comfy, kid." He brought the knife down hard on the table, and the handle stuck up straight out of the wood even after he released it. "You aren't goin' anywhere."

Ryan stopped struggling against his bonds. They wouldn't give an inch no matter which way he moved.

"Now," Steve said, "there's just one more thing I need." He walked over to Ryan and knelt to look Boss in the eye. "Where'd you hide your body?"

"It's of no further use to you," Boss retorted.

Steve wagged a finger. "I'll be the judge of that, furball. Now, out with it."

"No."

"Tell me, or else," Steve hissed, leaning in closer.

Boss seemed completely unfazed. "I won't tell you."

Steve gave Ryan a wink. "You just can't talk to some people, huh?" He stood, his eyes never leaving Ryan's. "Nothin' personal, kid. This is strictly business. I *am* a professional, after all."

Ryan opened his mouth to speak, but before he could form words, Steve socked him across the face. His head rocked to the left, the pain in his jaw so great it felt as if his soul had been batted from his body.

"Leave the boy out of this," Boss growled.

Steve grinned, raising a hand again. "Tell me where your body is."

"No."

Steve belted Ryan across the other side of the face, and Ryan's head jerked to the right. Warm liquid that tasted of copper drowned his tongue, a shrill ringing sound penetrating his ears. "I'm sorry, that is the incorrect answer," Steve said in a mock game-show host voice.

"Enough!" Boss roared. Steve struck Ryan again. Bodily liquid–Ryan guessed it was blood–dribbled from the corners of his mouth and from his nostrils. Boss shouted something else, but it sounded miles away. Whatever it was, it clearly hadn't been what Steve wanted to hear, because he decked Ryan in the face once more.

The ringing in Ryan's ears grew stronger. He spit blood onto the floor, struggling to keep his head upright. The room was spinning.

When the ringing in his ears finally began to dull, Ryan looked up, trying to focus on Steve, but his vision was red. *Is there blood in my eyes?* He blinked a few times, hoping the scarlet would clear. That only seemed to make things worse.

"I'm sure the kid can take a little more, don't you think?" Steve said, chuckling.

"Helsing, I'm begging y–"

Steve interrupted Boss by hitting Ryan again, and Ryan's vision faded in and out, the intensity of his pain reaching an all-time high, so extreme it was as though he were dreaming. The ringing in his ears returned, and his body felt light, weightless. He started to drift off, away from Steve, from Boss, from the agony. Boss screamed something, but Ryan couldn't decipher what.

I can't pass out right now, he thought, and focused on working through the pain. He willed himself to move his head. The slightest movement was excruciating; it felt as if a heavy rock were stuck inside his skull. It sent new shock waves through the muscles of his face, but still he pressed on. He forced his eyes open. It was hard to make out the sights before him, but he thought he saw Steve there.

What felt like an eternity passed before Ryan could hear Boss's and Steve's voices again. "When does it end, Helsing? How many innocent people must suffer because of your wicked path to revenge?"

Steve chortled. "My wicked path, huh? Let's not forget that you killed my big brother." Ryan's vision cleared some more. He saw Steve kneel, getting close to Boss. "I'll burn the earth, the people, and anything else standing between me and the bullet that'll finally take you out."

Boss narrowed his eye. "Killing me won't bring Alestair back."

"Maybe not. But damn, if it ain't fun to think about." Steve tilted his head. "Now, just to clarify. You said your body is under the tree in this brat's backyard?"

"Aye."

"If you're lying, you realize that wouldn't be in the kid's best interest?"

"I told you the truth. Now leave the boy be."

Steve nodded. "I love these talks of ours. You say the sweetest things." He blew a kiss to Boss before straightening himself and walking away.

The shape of his figure vanished from Ryan's blurry vision. Upstairs, a door slammed shut, and Boss released a heavy sigh. "Damn that man… We need to find a way out of here before he comes back."

"You… told him," Ryan croaked, his voice shaking.

Boss replied, but it sounded muffled. As he continued speaking, Ryan's surroundings faded away. Soon, he faded with them.

I'M TELLING YOU," Grey insisted, "I've seen her from somewhere. I might know who she is." He walked briskly through the forest, back from the way they'd come. Ronson followed close behind.

The other man laughed once. "I thought you said you *didn't* know who she is?"

Grey turned around. "I said I didn't remember her name and occupation, but I know I've seen that scar somewhere before. I just can't recall when and where."

"Well, thank goodness you were here to *not* recall such important details," Ronson said, a fake smile plastered on his lips.

Grey shot him a dirty look before turning back around, his thoughts racing as he tried to remember where he knew that woman from. Once she'd fallen into the river and vanished, he and Ronson had searched the bank, but she'd never reappeared. Then, after inspecting the rest of the surrounding area, they'd started the hike back.

"What about the eye?" Ronson asked out of nowhere.

"What?"

"The eye on the hood, Sheriff. Did that look familiar?"

Grey mulled over how much information he should give Ronson. Finally, he shook his head. "I don't think so." It was a lie, of course. But the last thing Grey wanted to discuss with the conspiracy-crazed Ronson was that damned eye. Truth be told, Grey *had* seen it before. Quite often, too.

Most remote areas in Twilight Peak had graffiti of an eye sitting inside a triangle that was a bit too small for it. It made Grey think of the Illuminati, although something about the symbol seemed different…

"You're lying," Ronson said way too matter-of-factly for Grey's liking. "But that's fine. Probably don't even know what it is, anyway."

"And you do?"

"Nope."

"Now *you're* the one who's lying."

Ronson snapped his fingers and pointed at Grey. "Hey, you're pretty good at that." Grey didn't reply, and as he stepped over a fallen tree, he decided he needed to keep his mouth shut for however much longer he'd be in Ronson's presence. "Whoever they are, I think they're tied to the curse somehow," Ronson added.

Grey scoffed. *I probably shouldn't humor him*, he thought. *But...* "The curse, huh?"

"Yes, the curse."

"And what is it that's cursed, exactly?"

"The town. *Our* town. How can you not know that?"

Grey rolled his eyes. "Explain something to me. How can the town be cursed when there's no such thing as curses?"

"I'm still trying to figure out how you didn't already know about Twilight Peak's curse," Ronson responded. "Especially considering how often people are attacked and killed just because."

Grey removed his flask from his jacket pocket and took a swig. The alcohol burned the back of his throat as it went down. "People die, Ronson."

"Not twice the average of other towns with the same population," Ronson replied triumphantly. "I would know. I keep my police scanner on. A majority of the calls you get are for attacks, murders, or missing persons. Strange animals, mysterious figures–pick your poison. It's all the same to me. The town is cursed. Has been ever since the witch died."

Grey returned the flask to his pocket. He needed more alcohol if he was going to be part of this conversation. It was true that there were a lot of deaths in Twilight Peak, but it was only cruel coincidence. Curses, magic, the supernatural–out of the question. "Yeah, well, at least you're right about one thing," Grey replied. "The town hasn't been the same since the 'witch' died. You say cursed, I say troubled."

"You're more than troubled if you've got a blood-soaked history like Twilight Peak does," Ronson muttered under his breath, and the tone in his voice told Grey he wasn't looking to argue the point further.

Without any idea how–or, quite frankly, the *want*–to continue this discussion, Grey kept his mouth shut as he marched on through the woods. *Just a bit farther, and I'm outta here.*

CHAPTER 7

CHYANN FOLLOWED WILLY INTO Ryan's garage and closed the door behind them as she glanced around. Up the steps to her right there was the broken window Willy had described. To her left, the cabinet and its toppled items he'd told her about.

"There're footprints by the front door," Willy said, jogging up the garage's steps. "I think that's where things started."

Chyann crossed her arms. "How could this happen? He was home for, like, five to ten minutes."

"I dunno. That's what I'm tryin' to figure out."

"I'm calling the cops." She pulled out her cell phone.

Willy stopped at the top of the stairs and spun

around to face her. "Whoa, hold on. Let's think about this for a second."

"I did," Chyann replied. "Unless you think Ryan was kidnapped by a werewolf, I'm calling the cops." She dialed 9-1-1, held the phone to her ear, and followed Willy up the stairs. He shook his head, stepping over broken glass into the house.

A moment later, they stood in the kitchen together. Chyann stared down curiously at the boot prints riddling the tiled floor, and an elderly woman's voice sounded on the other end of her call. "Twilight Peak Police Department. What's the nature of your emergency?"

"I think my friend was kidnapped," Chyann answered quickly. Just as the words escaped her lips, she spotted something next to the footprints–something with an odd coloration. She knelt over to inspect it.

"Oh my," the lady on the call said with a gasp. "What's the address? I'll have somebody over right away." But Chyann was barely listening now. Instead, she focused on the "something" she was looking at. It was a small object, oval-shaped and dark-green, with tiny white stripes streaking down the sides. Something about it gave her major déjà vu. "Ma'am, are you still there?"

"Chy," Willy whispered.

Chyann turned to face him. He knelt by the kitchen window, hiding behind the curtains and pointing at the yard with a horrified look on his face. Whatever he was seeing must have really freaked him out, but right now Chyann needed to focus on getting the authorities over here to investigate Ryan's disappearance. "Yes, sorry," she said to the lady on the phone. "1708 Ash Lane."

"Okay, I'll have somebody there as soon as possible," the woman promised.

"Thank you," Chyann replied, then hung up and lowered her cell. "What is it, Will?" She stepped up next to him and peered out the window. And, when she saw who stood outside, her jaw dropped. She ducked behind the curtain as well, a mixture of outrage and terror swirling furiously through her body. *It can't be*, she thought. *It can't, it can't, it can't.*

But it was. Steve Helsing strolled about Ryan's backyard, a shovel balanced on his shoulder, a smug grin plastered on his face. Even from inside, Chyann could hear him whistling a lighthearted tune. He sauntered over to the old oak tree at the edge of the yard and stared down at the ground beneath it.

"That prick's gotta be the one who took Ryan," Willy whispered.

Chyann shook her head. "How can that be? A building fell on top of him."

"Who cares? He's here now. I say we go and drop another one on him."

They watched as Steve stuck the blade of his shovel into the grass, as he tossed chunks of dirt over his shoulder.

Chyann snatched a knife from the block on the counter next to her. "Let's go."

Willy smiled, and Chyann led the way. Quickly and quietly they crept through the kitchen, into the

71

garage, and toward the backyard. When they reached the door leading outside, Steve still digging away with his back turned to them, the first thing she noticed was a cane in the yard's path, then that the gate was wide open.

Willy tiptoed across the pavement and picked up the cane. He glanced over his shoulder at Chyann and nodded. She readied the knife, nodding back. It was then that they began closing in on Steve. As they inched toward the man, Chyann's heart thudded against her ribcage.

Just as Chyann lifted the blade to attack, just as Willy raised the cane to swing, Steve stopped digging. He let out a tired sigh and stabbed the shovel into a dirt pile next to his hole. "You know, I had a feeling you two would be here." He pivoted and adjusted his hat. "I was really hoping that feeling was wrong, though."

*T*HE SIGHT OF his own truck made Grey sigh in relief. *I was afraid I'd never get out of there,* he thought. The trip back to Ronson's cabin had taken about thirty minutes, but it had felt so much longer to Grey.

The familiar sounds of static and voices sounded from his rolled-down window. Somebody must be trying to reach him.

"Sorry we didn't find more out there," Ronson said from behind Grey.

Grey couldn't tell if the apology was sincere or not, and he didn't really care. He'd been gone a long time; he needed to answer his radio. "Yeah, sure," he mumbled at Ronson, hurrying to his truck.

The radio blared to life once again as Grey threw open the vehicle door and grabbed his device from the holder. "Grey, do you read?" It was Griff. "Answer already! Over."

Grey lifted the radio to his mouth. "I'm here, Griff. What's goin' on? Over."

"Finally," Griff replied with a groan. "Doris just radioed me about a kidnapping at 1708 Ash Lane. Over."

1708? Isn't that...

Grey ran the back of his hand across his forehead, wiping the sweat away. "I'm forty minutes out, but if I speed I can make it in twenty. I'll meet you there. Over."

He set the receiver back on its holder and leaned against the open door for a moment. *Today just keeps throwin' me curveballs. I should've packed two flasks.*

"Don't forget our deal, Sheriff," Ronson said.

Grey turned around, peering at the other man from underneath his hat. "Why do you want the file?"

"Because," Ronson responded.

"Because why?" Grey pressed.

Ronson narrowed his eye at Grey as he spoke. "Hutton was a friend. 'Officially' he killed himself, but I don't think that's what really happened."

"Why?"

"Because he wasn't depressed!" Ronson shouted. "He didn't have any mental illnesses. He didn't even have a damn peanut allergy. There's no reason he would have–" Ronson stopped. His forehead wrinkled in frustration, and he sucked in a few breaths before continuing with a softer tone. "The week before he died, he told me he found something. Didn't say what it was. But the inventory of his possessions might give me an idea of what he discovered."

Grey's eyes went wide. *I'll be damned. Ronson just might be human after all.* He ran a palm across his stubble and opened his mouth to say something. However, he stopped short, catching sight of something that made chills race up and down his back.

Carved into the thick trunk of the tree growing closest to Ronson's cabin was the same eye and triangle Grey had seen spray-painted all over Twilight Peak.

Ronson seemed to notice Grey's surprise. He turned around, but when he saw the carving, he hardly reacted to it. "This is probably the third or fourth one they've put on my property," he said, waving a hand dismissively at the tree. "I'll buff it out in the morning."

Grey blinked a few times. "You serious?"

"Welcome to my world, Sheriff." Ronson rested his rifle on his shoulder and started back toward his cabin, disappearing through the security gate.

Grey chuckled nervously as he climbed into his truck and started the engine. *How the hell can he be so calm about something like that?*

However, there wasn't time to contemplate the matter further. He threw the stick into reverse and backed around before shifting into drive and flooring it.

He had somewhere important to be.

STOMACH CLENCHING, CHYANN stabbed the knife at Steve. He backstepped just in time to avoid the blade. She lunged forward and thrust the weapon once again, but Steve seized her arm. He twisted her wrist until she dropped the knife. Then he pulled her in and kneed her in the gut.

As all the air escaped her lungs and she gasped for breath, Steve punched her in the cheek. The force of the blow sent her face-first into the dirt. She rolled over, still trying to catch her breath, and saw Willy as he swung the cane at Steve. It struck the man in the shoulder.

Steve twirled around, caught the cane, yanked it from Willy, and started clobbering the boy with it. Bending down, Willy punched Steve in the groin. The man released a cry of pain, sinking onto the grass. Willy rose to meet Steve's jaw with another fist. Steve collapsed.

Willy reeled back to strike Steve once more. The man caught Willy's arm, wrenched him to the ground, and hit him over and over in the stomach. Still unable to breathe, Chyann watched in horror as her friend went motionless.

What felt like forever passed before she finally managed to get her breathing in order, but Steve was already up, shuffling back over to the hole he'd been digging. He mumbled angrily, though she couldn't make out what he was saying.

Steve grabbed the shovel and stabbed it into the earth, then tossed more dirt aside. All the while, Chyann struggled to climb to her knees, her head spinning. Being punched in the face wasn't something she was used to. She tried to stand, but the world seemed to tilt beneath her feet. She crashed to the ground.

"*What*?" Steve yelled. Chyann looked up at him. Once her vision adjusted, she could see the man stumbling out of the pit he'd created. "How?" He lowered his head, stroked his chin with his free hand. A second ticked by before his expression contorted into a vicious sneer. "That brat burned the body..." He shifted his attention to Chyann. "You stupid bitch. I can't get the cat out of your friend if I don't have a body to put his soul into!"

Chyann coughed a few laughs out. "Then I guess that means we get to keep him."

Steve held up the shovel, a murderous look in his eyes as he limped toward her. "You think this is funny?"

Sirens blared in the distance. Steve froze, glancing around in panic, and Chyann smiled, cocking her head. It sounded as though the sirens were heading this way.

Steve dropped the shovel. "You win this round, kid." He turned and hurried toward the back gate.

Chyann centered herself and attempted to stand, relief flooding her senses at the fact that Steve had left. She almost fell again but managed to keep herself upright. Beside her, Willy groaned and rolled over, moving his jaw as if testing whether it still worked properly. "Did we win?" he asked.

Chyann offered him a hand. He took it, and she helped him to his feet. "Steve's gone. Help me fill in this hole before the cops get here."

Willy tentatively rubbed his red cheek and glanced over at the newly formed crater. "What about Helsing?"

"We'll catch up to him." She grabbed the shovel and stared down into the makeshift grave. Charred bones poked out of the muck, Boss's skull staring up at her with empty black pits.

"What about Ryan?" Willy cried. "How do we know he's even still alive?"

As Chyann shoveled dirt back into the grave, she said, "Steve must have come here for Boss's corpse, which means he's trying to get Boss out of Ryan's body. *That's* how we know he's still alive."

WAKE UP, BOY!" Boss shouted. Ryan twitched as painful reality came crashing back to him. He cracked open his right eye, looked around the dark room. There was a soft glow hovering over the left side of his face, which indicated Boss's presence, but other than that he couldn't see anything. It probably didn't help that one of his eyes refused to open. *It must be swollen shut*, he thought, memories of the beatdown Steve had given him flooding his mind.

Every muscle in his face ached in ways he never could have imagined. This was by far the most severe pain he'd ever experienced.

"Hurry," Boss went on. "We have to leave."

Ryan tested his binds, but there wasn't the slightest bit of wiggle room. "I can't get free."

"*Try!*"

Ryan winced at the volume of Boss's voice. He was so loud… *Why's he gotta be stuck to the side of my face? It's like he's always screaming in my ear.* Still, Boss was right. They had to get out of here.

Ryan jerked his arms. The chair tipped slightly before shifting back to normal on the ground. *That might work.*

He rocked to the right, then to the left, back and forth, again and again. Finally, the chair tipped over. He held his breath, bracing himself for the pain, and smashed into the concrete floor.

The sound of wood splintering filled his ears. Despite the agony thundering through his skull, he couldn't help but smile as he pulled his arms free, slipping the ropes off his wrists and steadying himself.

He almost fell a few times, but he managed to balance himself against a wall and get to his feet. Using the wall to balance himself, he walked toward the stairs and began ascending them. Seven steps later, he reached the door, grabbed the knob, and turned it.

But the door refused to move.

"What's wrong?" Boss asked.

Ryan turned around and slid to the floor. "It won't open. Steve probably put something in front of it to block us from getting out."

There was a long pause before Boss replied. "Damn…"

"It's fine," Ryan said, wheezing.

"It's *not* fine. It's my fault you are here."

"Shut up. It's my own fault I'm here."

"Ryan…"

"I made the choice to not hand you over, and that was the right thing to do. I'm not gonna apologize for it, and neither should you."

Boss paused again before speaking. "Your stubbornness is going to get both of us killed."

Ryan let out a weak laugh. "Probably." He lifted a hand and gently ran his fingers over his cheeks. He must look awful. He could feel an abundance of bumps and crevices peppering his skin.

"What about down there?" Boss asked.

Ryan looked down into the basement at the pair of double doors. *Maybe there's another way out?* He gripped the stair railing, lifted himself up, and headed down the steps.

It wasn't long before he stood before the doors. They were tall, made of thick steel and wood, and covered in dust. Strange symbols were carved into them, none of which looked familiar.

He gripped one of the long doorknobs, its metal unnaturally cool to the touch, and turned it. As he did so, it *clunk*ed so loudly the sound echoed along the walls. He pushed the door open, and the other one swung agape at the same time as if of its own accord.

Ryan glanced at whatever lay beyond the doors. Saw mostly black. The faint glow Boss gave off illuminated the area a bit, but not enough to really see anything. Honestly, it was already dark in this basement, and Ryan had a feeling this part of it hadn't seen a shred of light in a very long time.

A strong, putrid odor assaulted Ryan's nostrils, and he resisted the urge to scrunch up his nose. It smelled of dust and rot, and he guessed that if Steve hadn't pounded his face in, the scent would be a lot stronger. "Man, that's gross," he said.

"What is this place?" Boss asked.

Ryan shrugged. "Not su–" His knee buckled. Without anything to grab in the open space, he fell to the cold, dirty floor. As he did so, his head struck something soft.

A creaking noise came from overhead, and although Ryan didn't know what the sound was, it made the hair on the back of his neck stand straight. He climbed to his hands and knees. Glanced up into the dark.

His sight was beginning to adjust, but even with the dim light Boss provided, he couldn't quite make out what he was staring at. More than anything, it looked like a dark mass floating above him. Tentatively, he stood and peered closer.

Realization came over him, and his heart stopped. Despite his hindered vision, there was no mistaking what he was looking at.

An eyeless, mummified human corpse hung by a rope tied around her neck. Her jaw hung wide open, a mop of gray hair clinging to her scalp.

Ryan screamed and fell backward onto the floor. "It's… it's…"

"What? Did you know them?" Boss asked.

Ryan couldn't speak. His thoughts were swirling so quickly that forming a coherent sentence wasn't possible. He *knew* where Steve had brought them now, and it was the last place he'd ever wanted to be.

"Ryan, she's dead. She is no threat to us." Boss said in a calming voice.

"We're… we're inside the witch's house!" He crawled away, as far as he could manage. He didn't want to be anywhere near that thing. There had always been talk regarding the legend of the witch, about how her body had been left in her basement to rot after authorities arrived and found her dead. Just like every other horror tale he'd heard, Ryan assumed the witch's story had been exaggerated in its retellings. But apparently, just like Adella Williams inhabiting the house Sadie moved into, it was true.

Ryan scrambled to his feet and spun around to get away. His plan was to shut these doors and find another way of escape; there was no chance he'd go searching in this room. Not with the witch's corpse hanging from the ceiling.

Just as he ran through the doorway, a fist collided with his stomach. He crumpled to the floor in a heap.

"You got outta your chair, little pig," Steve teased, standing over him. Ryan only sputtered in response, and Steve let out a low whistle as he stepped around him. "How the hell did you get in here? I couldn't get the door to budge."

Ryan watched as Steve pulled out his cell phone and switched on the flashlight, illuminating the room far better than before. Ryan glanced up at the corpse again.

Now he could see all the gruesome details.

The skin was pale, almost gray, and extremely dry, making it look like clay or paper-mache. It pulled tightly on the body, and it had even fallen off in some places, exposing parts of the teeth, skull, and bones. The corpse wore a ragged black tank top and jeans, and something that looked like a pile of cloth sat on the floor beneath her.

Sour bile rose in Ryan's throat. *This is a nightmare*, he thought. How was it even possible? How had the witch been so well-preserved for all these years? Had this room been so tightly shut and locked that not even bugs could get inside? From the way it smelled, he guessed that was the case, because it was clear no fresh air had gotten in.

Steve sauntered farther into the room and out of Ryan's sight. Ryan tried climbing to his feet, but his legs gave out beneath him, and he fell into a seated position. He gasped for breath, leaning against the doorway.

"Ryan, we have to move," Boss whispered.

Ryan shook his head. "I… can't."

Steve tsk-tsked, and Ryan looked around to find him. He stood next to a table housing a variety of bowls and jars.

The man held a jar in front of his flashlight to examine its contents. "You know, it was real stupid of you to torch the body, but that might not be an issue now." He set the jar down and lifted another to illuminate it. The containers were too far away for Ryan to see what was inside them, but Steve seemed interested in whatever they held. No, not interested. He seemed… impressed. "There is some serious black magic sitting in here," he said with a smile, then returned the jar to the table and gestured at the witch. "This broad was hard-core." He turned back to Ryan, his grin growing bigger as he went on. "Congrats, kid. You're about to be cat-free!"

CHAPTER 8

GREY CLIMBED OUT OF HIS TRUCK and shut the door behind him, and Griff met him at the end of the driveway of 1708 Ash Lane. "Situation's changed since the phone call," Griff said, pulling the notepad from his back pocket.

Grey furrowed his brow. "Changed how, exactly?"

"The kidnapper came back when the kids got off the phone," Griff said as he flipped through his notes. "And they know who he is."

"Let me guess. Is it our runaway from the hospital?"

"Hard to say for sure, but it seems like it, yeah."

Grey sighed and looked up at the two-story home. *The Myers house…* He was familiar with the family who lived here. And it wasn't for entirely good reasons, either. He walked up the pavement and into the garage, then made his way up a short flight of stairs and over some broken glass into the kitchen.

He rounded a corner and immediately recognized the two kids sitting at the kitchen table: Chyann Wakeman and Willy Wylee. Chyann's mother, Maddie, had once been Grey's deputy, long before Griff. Grey had met Chyann a handful of times, but he hadn't seen her since her mother quit the force and started a new career.

Willy, on the other hand, was part of many conversations back at the station. Or rather, his parents–Rick and Danica–were. Complaints regarding their constant fighting and shouting were almost as regular as Ronson's outlandish reports. Grey had crossed paths with Willy on a few isolated calls, but it was usually for minor theft or something equating to a slap on the wrist and a warning.

Grey examined the kids as he headed over to the table. *They both have bruised cheeks*, he thought, removing his hat and running his fingers through his short, dark hair. He rested his hat on the table before pulling out a chair and sitting across from Chyann and Willy.

"Sheriff Greyson," Chyann said in greeting.

Grey nodded. "Good to see you again, kid. How's your mom?"

"Busy," she answered.

Grey nodded a second time. "So, fill me in on what happened."

Chyann cleared her throat. "Ryan is missing. Initially, we didn't know what happened to him, but right after I called the station, a man broke into the backyard. He's..." She trailed off and shared a look with Willy before speaking again. "He's tried kidnapping us before."

"He *did* kidnap us before," Willy corrected her.

Grey sat for a moment and rubbed his chin with his knuckles. "What's this guy look like?"

Willy leaned forward. "Brown hair, a hat, and a long coat that makes him look like a jackass."

Chyann jerked in her seat and Willy twitched in his. Grey guessed she had just kicked his leg under the table. "Will," she hissed. Willy crossed his arms and looked away.

"His name is Steve Helsing," Chyann said, turning back to Grey.

Grey lowered his hand. "As in *Van* Helsing?"

Chyann waved a hand dismissively. "I know how it sounds, but I swear that's his name."

"Why's he after you guys?" Grey asked.

"I have no idea!" Chyann exclaimed, suddenly seeming flustered. "Probably because he's a psychopath who enjoys killing teenagers?"

Grey reached into his pocket, noting her sarcasm, and retrieved his cell phone. He pulled up the security footage from this morning and showed it to the teens. "This the guy?"

They stared at the screen for the duration of the video. When it concluded, Chyann said, "The video's a little dark, but it definitely looks like him."

Grey lowered the phone and faced Griff. The deputy nodded. Their "shadow man" and Ryan's kidnapper were most likely one and the same.

"The man in this security footage stole his truck out of my impound lot early this morning," Grey said, looking at Chyann once again. "He was in the hospital for some time after being found under a collapsed building." Chyann averted his gaze. Grey couldn't be sure, but she seemed... guilty. Grey filed the thought away and continued. "Any idea where he might have taken Ryan?"

Willy leaned back in his seat. "You think we'd be sittin' on our asses talkin' to you if we did?"

Grey snorted. "If I had to guess, I'd say you two tried jumping him when he came strolling through the backyard." He motioned at Willy's face. "Judging by the bruises, that didn't go over well, huh?"

Willy sneered, while Chyann looked down with embarrassment. Grey let the silence hang for a moment before rising to stand. "Now, if you two will excuse me, I gotta go make an important call." He put his hat back on. "Don't go anywhere. I've still got questions."

He turned his back on them and followed Griff from the room to the garage. Once they were out of earshot, Griff tapped Grey on the shoulder. "So, what do you think?"

Grey opened his coat and pulled his flask out. "About the great-grandson of the guy-who-killed-Dracula kidnapping a kid?" He untwisted the cap and lifted it to his lips. "Doesn't sound crazy at all."

He downed the remainder of the flask before putting the lid back on. The alcohol had gone down a little easier than his last heavy swig back in the woods, but it burned all the same.

"Going a little hard on the whiskey today, huh?"

Grey chuckled. "What are you? A cop?"

Griff grinned a bit, but Grey could see the concern on his face. "You gonna need me to drive you back to the station again?"

"Nah," Grey said with a headshake. "I'm still good."

Griff's cheeks twitched, and Grey had a feeling he intended to press further. He knew Grey sometimes drank on duty, and he'd always been against it. However, rather than insisting on discussing the issue, he crossed his arms and said, "Weird name or not, this 'Helsing' guy's description matches our truck thief."

Grey bit his lip. "Go follow up with those two and call a couple of our lab geeks over here to sweep." He put his flask away and pulled out his cell phone. *I'm not looking forward to this next part*, he thought, then shook the device at Griff and said, "I gotta make a call."

"Good luck." Griff headed back into the house.

Grey pivoted and unlocked his phone. It took a bit of scrolling through his contacts, but eventually he found the entry for Paige Myers. Her name on the screen may as well have had cobwebs on it. They hadn't spoken in some time, and the last time they had, it hadn't been the most friendly.

Grey tapped her name, revealing both her personal number and the number to the hospital, and his thumb hovered over the call button for the hospital.

The last thing she'd want to hear was that her son was missing, and to add insult to injury, it would be coming from Grey of all people. He mentally prepared himself for the task at hand and tapped the green phone symbol. *Here goes nothing, I guess.*

It wasn't long before somebody picked up, and he requested to speak to Paige. He was put on hold, forced to listen to an upbeat jingle while he waited. Just as the music looped, there was a *click*, and a voice Grey knew all too well spoke. "Hello?"

"Paige, it's Grey." He paused so she could respond. Continued when she said nothing. "I'm at your place right now. The station got a call for a possible kidnapping, and… your son, Ryan, has been kidnapped."

"What?" Paige cried. "How? What happened?"

"That's what I'm trying to figure out. His friends have an idea of who took him, so we just need to find out where he could be."

"I'm coming home," she said quickly. Grey opened his mouth to assure her she didn't need to, but the line *click*ed as she hung up on him. *Great, this is just what I need.*

He pocketed his phone and rubbed his tired eyes. *I* definitely *should'a packed a second flask.*

RYAN STRUGGLED AGAINST his new bindings as Steve sorted through a pile of various items and ingredients on the table. The man whistled gently, moving things from one side to the other and flipping through a dusty book, which he had also found inside the sealed room. Dim candlelight illuminated Steve and his workspace as he continually shifted around.

Since Ryan had broken the chair, Steve had tied his wrists to the thick wooden beams beneath the staircase. His bindings were just as tight as before, holding both arms high above his head, and they left no room to wiggle his hands free.

Steve paused, staring down at a page in the book. He grabbed a knife and bowl and turned to approach Ryan. "If you'd be so kind," he said with a smile. When he reached Ryan's side, he snatched the boy's hand, twisted it over to expose the palm, and sliced the flesh open. Ryan winced at the stinging pain. It was nothing compared to Steve's beatings, but it still hurt.

Steve closed Ryan's fingers and squeezed so that blood would drip into the bowl. "So how about it, kid?" he began. "You regretting your choices yet?" Ryan remained silent, and Steve went on. "You could have avoided all this if you would'a just worked with me the first go-around." Apparently satisfied with the amount of blood in the bowl, Steve released Ryan and swished the liquid around. "It's no good for either of us in the long run, y'know? I have to beat you half to death, you have to get *beaten* half to death. I mean, honestly." He raised an arm in a pleading manner. "Who wins here?"

He ambled over to the table to resume his work. As he did so, there was a soft flash of light in front of Ryan's face, and Boss appeared once again. "Don't pretend that you feel guilty about this," he hissed at Steve.

Steve shook his head and laughed some more. "Oh, I don't." He turned and pointed at them. "But you might. You killed Alestair, and now you're the reason this poor kid is about to die, too." He gave Boss a serious look and continued in a sarcastic, growly voice as though mocking Boss's own. "Tell me, how many innocent people must suffer because of your wicked path to *escape*?"

Boss huffed. "You won't be able to remove me if you kill the boy."

"Well, duh!" Steve exclaimed, rolling his eyes. "I think we've already established that, you moron. I'm talking about the *ritual* I'm preparing."

Ryan lifted his head. *Ritual?* he wondered. *What ritual?*

Steve seemed to notice Ryan's reaction, a sinister grin forming on his lips. "Yeah. Spoiler alert, kid. You probably won't live through this. You of all people should know that having a soul pulled out of your body doesn't *tickle*." He motioned at Ryan with a free hand. "You got lucky before. That amulet you two used was called *Shi*, and soul stuff was kind of its specialty." He lifted a jar, twisted off the top, and dumped the grime into the bowl holding Ryan's blood. "Then you had to go and *smash* it," he added with vexation.

Boss sighed tiredly. It took a while for him to respond to Steve. "You've already killed me once," he finally said. "Why not just take my bones to your family? Prove to them that you killed me. Leave me to exist in this state for the remainder of my days."

Steve turned, the expression on his face suddenly blank. "No."

"And why not?"

"Because you killed my brother. You struck him down in cold blood–while he was asleep, no less–and I'm going to make you suffer for it."

The accusation lingered in the air, the tension between Boss and Steve so great it was palpable. But what Steve said about Boss killing his brother–it couldn't be true, could it? The more time Ryan spent with Boss, the less Steve's claims seemed plausible.

Ryan tried to open his mouth to speak, but it felt stiff and heavy. His throat burned, and only a thin hiss managed to escape his lips. *"Boss,"* he thought, *"you didn't actually kill his brother, right?"*

He wasn't sure if he wanted the truth, but it was a question that needed to be answered. When Boss finally replied, Ryan's blood froze in his veins.

"I'm afraid it's true," Boss said in Ryan's head. *"I killed Alestair Helsing."*

*C*HYANN SAT NEXT to Willy at the kitchen table in Ryan's house. Deputy Griff had returned a few minutes earlier, but he'd told them not to move as he slipped into the hall to make some more calls. The aches in her sore, swollen cheek flared as she grit her teeth in frustration, but the pain was nothing compared to how worried she was for Ryan.

"Can't believe we're sittin' on our asses instead of chasin' Steve," Willy grumbled.

"But Grey can help us this time," Chyann replied. "We're not dealing with a ghost. We're dealing with a guy."

Willy threw his hands in the air. "He doesn't even believe half the stuff we've told him!" Chyann reached out to put a hand on Willy's shoulder, but he yanked himself away from her and leaned against the table. "I'd be out there right now if I had any freakin' clue where to start," he said.

Once he stilled, Chyann rested a hand on his back, trying to comfort him. She knew how he was feeling; she didn't like sitting here and waiting around any more than he did. Also, she had no doubt that if they knew where Steve could be hiding, they would have already left to…

Her fingers brushed something small and scratchy on Willy's sweatshirt, pulling her from her thoughts. She knit her brow and plucked the object from the fabric.

The thing was oval-shaped and dark-green, with three white stripes streaking down the front of it, and she recalled seeing something just like it when she'd arrived at Ryan's house earlier. Now that she had time to inspect it, she did just that. Quickly, she realized it was a seed. One that stuck to fabric easily. And it seemed so familiar…

I know I've seen seeds like this somewhere before to-day. But where? She knew she hadn't spotted one in a while, not since she was a kid. If she remembered correctly, she used to pull them off the bottom of her pants all the time.

A single location came to mind, and she thought, *Oh, no.* It was a horrifying realization, but it made too much sense to not be correct.

"I think I know where Ryan is," she whispered.

Willy turned back to her with his full attention. "I'm all ears." He looked down and noticed the seed in her hand. "The hell is that?"

"It's a seed of a flower called Black Cat's Bloom."

"Okay?"

"We used to get these stuck to our pants all the time out in the woods."

"Okay, I get that. But what's it got to do with Ryan?"

"Black Cat's Bloom is a super rare flower that only grows here in Twilight Peak. Specifically all around the Worthrow house."

The color drained from Willy's face. "Steve took Ryan to the witch's house?"

"This was stuck to your back," Chyann explained, holding up the seed. "Maybe it fell off of Steve earlier in the yard. There was also one in here that I saw when I called the cops."

"So Steve's been dragging them into town whenever he leaves his hideout."

"Exactly."

Willy hopped out of his seat. "Well, what're we waitin' for, then? Let's bounce."

Just as Chyann got up, Deputy Griff returned from the hallway. He lowered his phone and put it back in his pocket. He stopped when he noticed the two of them on their feet. "Stretching your legs?"

"We know where Ryan is," Chyann blurted.

Griff offered a skeptical look but said nothing, and Grey strode into the room from the garage. "The kids think they know where their friend is," Griff told him.

Grey looked at Chyann curiously. "Yeah?"

"He's at the Worthrow house," Chyann said.

Grey's expression morphed into one of disbelief. "Why would you assume that, pray tell?"

Chyann showed him the seed. "This is a seed for a rare flower that grows on the property. None of us have been there since we were kids, but that must be where it came from."

Grey seemed to mull over that information for a bit. When he looked at Chyann again, she could tell he didn't believe her theory. "So you're saying that your friend is being held hostage at the witch's house because you found a seed? Bit of a jump, don't you think?"

Chyann lowered her arm. "You got any better ideas?"

"There's a tall iron fence surrounding the Worthrow property," Grey replied. "I highly doubt that guy got himself and your friend over it. Stay here. We'll have more help soon, and we'll figure out where they are. Until then, I can't have you two out and about."

"But–"

"Don't make me handcuff you to the table," Grey interrupted her. "I already have one pissed off mom on her way here. I don't need two of 'em, all right?"

Chyann opened her mouth to protest, but decided to stay silent. Grey pointed at the chairs. "Park it."

Chyann balled her fists at her sides, the seed scratching her palm as she crushed it in her grip. Defeated, she turned around and sat back down. Willy did the same, muttering under his breath angrily.

Grey gestured at Griff, and the two went back into the garage.

Once they disappeared, Chyann glanced over at Willy. Locking eyes, they nodded at one another. *If Grey won't listen*, Chyann thought, *we'll just have to save Ryan ourselves.*

CHAPTER 9

RYAN SAT WITH HIS EYES CLOSED, listening as Steve worked away. The man casually whistled the tune of a pop song–one Ryan couldn't remember the name of–as though he were baking cookies rather than preparing to perform an evil, soul-sucking ritual.

Even so, Ryan's thoughts drifted back to the last thing Boss had said before he'd faded away earlier.

"I killed Alestair Helsing."

Ryan didn't believe it. He couldn't. He'd only known Boss for a short time, but cold-blooded murder didn't seem like something he was capable of.

Ryan thought back to the day they'd met, recalled the way Boss had nearly won the fight against Steve before being fatally wounded. He'd certainly had no problem with killing then. Was that instance any different from the one with Steve's brother?

As Ryan wrestled with the morality of it all, Steve's whistling stopped. "It's showtime, kitties and gents!"

Ryan forced open an eye. A large pentagram-type symbol had been drawn on the floor in blood. Candles had been placed at the symbol's points, bathing the room with an ominous red glow.

"Now, I know what you're thinking," Steve started, raising a finger. "'Mr. Helsing, my face hurts. Can you make this quick'? You might also be thinking that I can't do this without a body to send your pet into. That's the beauty of it–I don't need one!" He turned and retrieved a jar from the table. "What you see here is a regular old jar, but this symbol I carved into the lid"–he lowered the top to show Ryan–"gives it the power to hold my hopes and dreams. Maybe even a soul or two, if I do my ritual work properly."

Steve removed the lid, placed the jar in the center of the pentagram-type symbol, and clapped his hands. "All right, let's get this show on the road, shall we?"

GREY STUCK HIS head through the open garage door. The other officers and lab techs had to be on their way soon. As evening took hold of the sky, the air began to chill, a breeze whistling through another one of the doorways.

Griff cleared his throat, and Grey turned to face

him. "What do we think about the old house?" Griff asked. "Could our guy be hiding out there?"

Grey shrugged. "Those flowers are all over the woods, and we already know he was in the area."

"Isn't the road to the house blocked off? How could he have found it when it's so far away?"

Grey scratched his cheek and leaned against a wall. "No idea. The only stops on that road are a gas station and a few…" Grey trailed off, realization slamming into him like a truck. How had he not realized it earlier?

The road with the turnoff to the Worthrow house had a gas station–the same gas station their suspect had robbed this morning.

"What is it?" Griff asked.

Grey pulled out his phone and brought up a map of town. He tapped on the screen until he found the rest stop in question, then showed the device to Griff. "This is the gas station he robbed." He slid the screen to the left, into the woods. "This is where the house is located." He slid the map upward and pressed on an area next to the river. "And this is where Ronson saw him." Grey zoomed out to show how the areas were in close proximity. "The kid was right. That house might be where our guy is hiding."

Griff raised his radio. "I'll call it in."

Grey started up the steps leading back into the house. "Tell them to meet us at the Worthrow property, and quick." He could hear Griff's radio buzz with static even as he entered the kitchen. "Okay, you two, come with–" He rounded the corner and stopped in his tracks. No one sat at the table; Chyann and Willy were gone.

A breeze rolled through the room, and Grey looked over to find the curtains of an open window swaying back and forth.

*C*HYANN'S CHEST BURNED as she struggled to keep up with Willy, a blur of green trees and brush on her every side as she ran farther into the woods.

Willy seemed to easily remember their old path to the Worthrow house, so Chyann let him lead. They sprinted past the crooked gray tree and the huge white boulder, soon stumbling out onto the remote dirt road.

Gasping for breath, they stopped for a few moments. Willy coughed and patted his chest, then turned left and dashed on.

Chyann put her hands behind her head, still trying to catch her breath. "Will, wait a minute." She sucked in as much air as she could before hurrying after him. "Slow down! We need a plan! We can't just barge in there."

"Oh, yeah?" Willy shouted at her. "Well, lucky for you, I've already got a plan." He paused to snatch up a thick tree branch almost as large as a baseball bat. "After we 'barge in there,' I'm gonna put Helsing back in the hospital."

"I'm being serious!" Chyann scolded, reaching his side.

"You're right. I'm just kiddin'. I'm gonna put him in the graveyard, instead."

Chyann grabbed him by the shoulders. "We have no idea what Steve has planned. For all we know, we could be heading into a trap. Don't forget that this is *Samantha Worthrow's* house."

"Ding Dong, Chy," Willy said, pushing her hands away. "Last time I checked, the witch was definitely dead. I'm not worried about her. I'm worried about Steve." He pivoted to continue running. "You can help me, or you can stay here. Not like you wanna be involved, anyway."

Chyann stomped in front of him, blocking his path. "What the hell is *that* supposed to mean?"

"You're only helpin' now 'cause you feel guilty."

"Did it ever occur to you that I'm the only one who seems to understand how dangerous monster hunting is? Did you also forget that *I'm* the one who figured out how to stop Adella? That *I'm* the one who got stabbed by the psycho puppet and nearly fell off the roof of the theater? I'm helping now because Helsing has Ryan, not because I feel guilty about anything."

"Okay, great. What about tomorrow? Next week? Once we have Ryan back, that doesn't mean somethin' else won't stick its ugly head outta the sand. When that happens, are you just gonna go back to tryin' to talk us outta this 'cause you're too scared?"

"Too scared?" Chyann screamed at him. "Why wouldn't I be 'too scared'? Do you think any other well-adjusted kid is going to respond differently when they find out monsters are real?"

"You're not 'well-adjusted,'" Willy yelled back. "None of us are. My folks hate me, Ryan's dad's behind bars, and your..." He trailed off, shifting his weight. "Cassidy."

Chyann looked away as she blinked back tears. They were both upset, their emotions running high. That's all this was. He didn't mean what he said, and even if he did, she didn't intend on listening to him.

"I think this *is* all about Cassidy," he added.

"Will, don't–"

He brandished his stick at her. "You're not scared you'll wind up missin' like she did, are you? You're scared you'll find out what really happened to her. You wanna go back to not knowin' anything about all this!"

"You don't know what you're talking about." She wiped the moisture from her eyes.

Willy lowered the branch. "Maybe not, but I do know *you*." He let the words linger before he rested the stick on his shoulder and jogged on.

Chyann rubbed her eyes to clear any remaining tears, then took a deep breath and followed him.

Soon they quickened their pace, sprinting down the road. Finally, they reached the end of it.

The Worthrow house stood as large and intimidating as ever, its two second-story windows giving it the appearance of a sinister face. A tall brick chimney rose from the house's left side, but at only a fraction of the original height. A lot of the chimney had broken away due to years of disrepair and bad weather. Whatever paint had originally coated the building was nearly gone now, leaving its color a pale gray-brown. Thorn-covered vines curled and twisted up the house's sides and into exposed holes in the wood. A tall, wrought iron fence surrounded the property, spikes jutting out of the top of each post.

The only way past the fence was through a gate at the front of the property that was chained and locked shut—at least, it should have been. As Chyann and Willy approached the fence, Chyann saw that the gate hung slightly ajar. A pile of rusted chains and broken padlocks lay on what had once been an impressive cinder block path.

Willy offered his branch to Chyann. Before she could protest, he said, "You're not goin' in there without somethin' to smash Steve's head with."

Chyann pushed the stick back toward him. "Neither are you." She searched the ground and decided on taking a piece of the iron fence. Rust had developed on the base of the post, and over time it must have broken off and fallen to the ground. She lifted it from the brush and wiped away some of the dirt and grass covering it.

She turned the metal over in her hands. It seemed reliable enough to take inside. When she glanced over at Willy, he raised his branch. "Ready?"

Chyann's heart raced, her palms growing slippery with sweat. She'd been sure that Steve was here, but where was his truck? She couldn't see it anywhere. *Maybe that's the idea*, she thought. *He probably knows the police are searching for it, so he took the time to park it in a hidden spot.*

"Chy?" Willy's voice speared through her thoughts.

She turned to him and held up the fence-piece. "I'm ready."

Without another word, Willy trudged through the open gate, and, when they reached the front door, shoved open the rotting wood and led them into the dark.

*G*REY GRIPPED THE steering wheel tightly as he drove his truck toward the witch's house, trees lining the road as far as the eye could see.

Griff sat in the passenger seat. The deputy lowered his cell phone, ending his call with the station. "Deputies are redirecting to the old house."

"Good." Grey scanned the left of the roadside.

"Some of the guys sounded spooked when I told them where we're headed. This place must be pretty grim, huh?"

"You know what happened there, don't you?"

"Of course. I don't have all the details, but I know it was bloody."

Grey cleared his throat. "That's putting it mildly."

"I'll say. Seventeen murdered children? That's horrific."

"Seventeen kids were found in her basement," Grey said. "But there's at least twenty to thirty other kids that went missing around the time Worthrow was around. Hard to say exactly how many of the vanishings she was responsible for, though."

Griff pondered the information before responding. "You lived in Twilight Peak when it happened, didn't you?"

"I was in my senior year of high school when the news broke," Grey answered, his chest growing tight. "Took the sheriff at the time a while before he caught on to her."

"She killed herself, right?"

"Yeah. Nobody knows for sure whether she knew she'd been caught or if she just wanted to do it. By the time authorities got to the scene, she was hanging from a beam in her basement."

"And legend has it, she's still down there?"

"That's more than just legend," Grey replied. "The sheriff was so disgusted and furious with her, he refused to let anyone touch her body. One of the first kids she killed was his little boy. I guess he figured leaving her the way she'd been found was the closest thing he could get to revenge."

Grey slowed down and pulled the truck over on the side of the road, then undid his seat belt and climbed out of the vehicle.

Griff scrambled out after him, and they headed toward the house.

Unfortunately, the path was overgrown with thick plant life that the truck couldn't get through. They'd have to go on foot the rest of the way.

"They took down the signs here, the ones indicating the turnoff to her house," Grey explained. "They even locked up the building so curious townsfolk couldn't get in."

Griff stepped up next to Grey as they walked through the trees. "It's a bit much, isn't it?" Griff asked. "Locking up the building? Leaving the body to rot? What was the sheriff thinking?"

Grey pushed a branch out of his way. "The guy wasn't really the same after they found his kid. He didn't stay sheriff much longer after Worthrow died, either. To be honest, if I'd have seen the bloodbath he did, I would've quit the force, too. He didn't tell anyone about leaving her down there; he just assured the town she was dead. Rumors started to spread about what he did, but most folks figured that even if it were true, it wasn't worth raising a fuss over."

Grey found the path leading up to the house, and he was surprised to see that despite years of no use, it remained visible. Grass and other brush sprouted up through the flat, dry dirt, and bright-purple flowers stood tall amongst the rest of the weeds. *Black Cat's Bloom*, he thought.

They stepped over blossom after blossom as they trekked down the path, and soon Grey spotted the witch's house up ahead. The sight sent electricity arcing up and down his spine.

The witch had been the boogeyman of Twilight Peak for years, and he was about to stroll right on up to her front door.

*R*YAN SAT QUIETLY with his hands above his head. The bindings had begun to slice into his wrists, and he had to keep flexing and wiggling his fingers to keep the blood flowing through them.

Boss hovered over the left side of Ryan's face, and Steve chanted from his position across the room. The chant consisted of ancient-sounding words Ryan didn't understand, and as Steve shouted it, the candles' flames flickered. Whole minutes passed, and Steve started to speak faster.

An odd feeling brewed in Ryan's chest. It felt as if someone had their hand in his ribcage and was attempting to guide him toward Steve. The more Steve chanted, the stronger the sensation grew.

Boss's form began to glow red. Whatever Steve was doing, it was having an effect.

The bowl on the floor trembled, and the ingredients inside burst into flames. The fire grew higher, higher, higher, burning white-hot, and Ryan struggled against his bindings. He had to get free, had to stop this, because if what Steve said was true, this ritual wouldn't just separate Ryan and Boss. It could very well be lethal.

Steve's words grew even faster, even louder, and the flames grew with them. Ryan's chest flared with searing pain. Still, he fought against his bindings until he felt them loosen.

The pain in both Ryan's chest and in his wrists reached a crescendo, and he screamed. All the while, Steve bellowed the last bit of his chant.

Finally, Ryan freed himself. He fell face-first to the floor. The flames of the candles went out. The only light that remained was the scarlet glow around Boss.

Slowly, Boss's illumination faded. As it disappeared, so did the strange sensation in Ryan's chest. He let out several relieved breaths as he picked himself up off the dirty floor.

"What?" Steve shrieked. Ryan raised his head, saw a panicked Steve searching over his ritual ingredients. "No. No no no! It should have worked!"

"Maybe you're just bad at this," Ryan said, coughing.

Steve looked away from the pentagram-type symbol to glare at Ryan. "I was *raised* to do this."

Boss laughed. "That does not mean you cannot be 'bad' at it, as Ryan so eloquently puts it."

"Actually," Steve began, rising to his feet, "I'm not. This means the magic that stuck you two together can't be undone." He stomped over to Ryan, snatched him by the shirt, and lifted him up. "And you went and smashed that amulet, you little moron!"

Steve shook Ryan and slammed him into the wall. Ryan writhed in Steve's grasp, and the man raised his fist to punch.

It was then that Boss vanished, that Ryan's eyes began to glow yellow.

Steve tried to strike Ryan, but Ryan involuntarily jerked his head to the side. *Boss must have taken over*, he realized, and Steve's fist collided with the brick behind his head. Steve recoiled, howling in pain, and Boss made Ryan uppercut the man. Steve stumbled backward at the force.

Boss made Ryan start running, but Steve caught Ryan's arm, yanked him to the floor, and landed a blow to his cheek. In an instant, the yellow glow emanating from his eyes dissipated.

Steve punched Ryan again, then grabbed him by the collar and pulled him close. "I hope he can feel your pain," the man hissed, and reeled back to launch another blow.

CHAPTER 10

RYAN COVERED HIS FACE WITH HIS arms as Steve punched him over and over.

"You're gonna die down here!" Steve yelled. "And for what? That slimy fur bag renting out the empty space in your head?" Steve seized Ryan's arms and pushed them down. "You like bein' a hero? Look at where that got you!" He belted Ryan in the cheek. Ryan's head jerked to the side, pain clouding his senses.

This is it, he thought. *Helsing's gonna beat me to a pulp.* He braced himself for the next hit, forcing an eye open. Steve readied a fist, but before he could swing, what looked like a club slammed into the side of his skull. Steve toppled over, his hat flying off his head.

Willy stood before them, holding what Ryan realized to be a large stick. Chyann appeared and knelt at

Ryan's side. She carefully slipped a hand around him and helped him sit up. "Are you okay?"

He nodded, though his body throbbed with aches and pains. "I'll live."

"You *brat*," Steve hissed. He stood, touching his fingers to the side of his head. When he pulled his hand away, they were stained a dark red. He glared at Willy. "Round two, huh, Peewee?"

Willy brandished his branch, offering Chyann a quick backward glance. "Get Ry outta here."

"I'm not leaving you down here with that psycho," Chyann retorted. Ryan tried to stand, faltering, but she helped to steady him.

"I'm not in a very good mood right now," Steve began. "So either you get out of my way, or you die."

"Come over here and kill me then," Willy said.

Steve chuckled, offering Willy a little wave. "Oh, you! I guess since you asked so nicely."

The man lunged forward, and Willy swung the stick. Steve stepped back, avoiding the blow. When he rushed at Willy again, the boy hit high. Again, Steve backed up.

Three, four, five times they "danced" like this. On the last time, Steve leaned forward rather than backward. Willy swung early. At the opening, Steve dove for Willy and snatched the branch. They struggled back and forth until Steve threw Willy against the wall.

Willy fell to the floor, dazed and weaponless. Steve turned toward Ryan and Chyann. Chyann stepped in front of Ryan and raised her hands.

Steve tapped the top of the stick against his chin. "I feel like this has happened before." He raised the branch and swung wildly. Chyann ducked and spun beneath the attack, bringing her leg up, and kicked Steve in the face. The blow knocked him toward Willy.

As Steve stumbled back, Willy leapt to his feet. He tackled the man to the floor and punched him in the cheek. He struck Steve twice more, but the man covered his face. As Willy reeled back for another attack, Steve smacked the boy on the side of the head, shoved him off, and jumped into a standing position.

Willy started to get up, but Steve rammed into him, shoved him into the wall again, and punched him across the face. Willy fell sideways but managed to stay on his feet. Steve punched him a second time. Willy toppled over. Steve picked him up and continued striking him.

Chyann rushed from Ryan's side toward the fight. Steve must have anticipated this, because he turned sharply and threw Willy at her. The pair crashed to the floor in a heap.

Chyann tried to move, but Steve was too quick. He booted her in the face. Her head slammed into the floor, and Steve pressed his shoe against the side of her skull. She screamed as he put his weight on her.

Breath catching in his throat, Ryan tried to think of a way to help his friends. He spotted the branch a few feet away from him, then stumbled over to it, scooped it up, and readied it to swing. All the while, Chyann's screaming grew louder. Just as Ryan attacked, Steve spun around.

The club rammed into Steve's head with a *clunk*. He staggered backward, freeing Chyann, but the blow gained Ryan little reprieve. Within seconds Steve regained his balance and charged for Ryan. At the same time, a yellow glow began to emanate from Ryan's eyes, and his whole body went numb.

Boss made Ryan dodge Steve's attack, then had him slam the stick into the man's stomach. Steve sputtered and sent his fists through the air. Boss made Ryan strike Steve in the jaw, avoiding the man's every blow.

Steve caught his balance and faced Ryan. Boss made Ryan swing the branch downward. Steve caught Ryan's wrist and Spartan kicked the boy in the gut.

The yellow glow faded from Ryan's eyes as he fell back-first into the double doors behind him. They split open, and he landed hard on the cold granite floor, right beneath the hanging corpse of the witch. Steve pounced on top of him and cracked a fist across his cheek several times.

Ryan spit up blood. Steve grasped his shirt collar and shook him violently. "Come out here and look me in the eye. Stop hiding behind the kid!"

There was a flash, and Boss appeared.

Steve gave Boss a crazed smile. "Congratulations, pussycat. You get to die." He moved his hands from Ryan's shirt to the boy's throat and squeezed. Immediately, Ryan began losing oxygen. His pulse pounded in his ears as he tried to speak, but all that came out was a choking noise. "I want you to look me in the eye while the kid dies," Steve went on. "I want the last thing both of you think is that it's all *your* fault."

Ryan kicked and squirmed. Steve held firm. Ryan reached out, trying to find something, *anything* to help, as Steve kept squeezing his throat.

Boss glared up at Steve, grunting. "My body is gone. You have nothing to return home with. You failed to separate the boy and I, and now you've resorted to killing us for pride's sake." Steve's smile faltered ever so slightly. Ryan's fingers caught something nearby, and although his vision had begun to darken, he grabbed onto it. "But how you kill me," Boss continued, "whether it be quickly and painlessly or slowly and horribly–it doesn't matter. Taking my life will no longer bring meaning to your own."

Steve frowned, his eyebrows knitting together, and Ryan pulled the object he'd grabbed toward himself. It was cool against his fingertips and felt round in shape. *It must be one of the jars*, he thought. With the last of his energy, he tightened his grip on the jar, raised it high, and smashed it into Steve's face.

Glass shattered, and Steve's grip on Ryan's neck loosened. Ryan rolled away and sucked in several deep breaths. Someone grabbed his arms and hauled him to his feet. When he looked to see who it was, he found Chyann and Willy holding him.

"Why?" Steve asked from behind them. Ryan and his friends turned around. Steve rose to his feet; he stood between the three of them and the double doors. He wiped broken glass from his now-bleeding face. "Why is there always some roadblock whenever I get close? I swear, you three are worse than…" He trailed off. Smiled. "Magnus," he whispered, and pointed at

Boss. "That's why you came to Twilight Peak. This is where the old codger lived."

"Aye," Boss replied.

Ryan lifted his head–it felt heavier than ever–and looked at Steve. "I guess being a roadblock runs in the family."

What seemed like whole minutes passed, and no one said anything. Finally, Steve threw his hands in the air, bursting into a fit of laughter. "Of course! It all makes sense now. You're the grandkid he never shut up about." Steve continued cackling, the sound filling the basement, and chills ran up Ryan's spine.

Finally, Steve calmed. "Honestly, that's fine by me! I hated the bastard, and you know what, Boss?" He reached into his coat and pulled out a familiar silver colt. "It's gonna make me extra happy to not only put a bullet in you, but to also put a bullet in what's left of Magnus's family." He aimed the gun at Ryan, and Boss disappeared. Steve pulled the hammer back. "So much for killing you not mattering, huh?"

Ryan took Chyann's and Willy's hands and squeezed. *What do we do now? We're cornered, and Steve has–*

"Drop the gun," a man's voice commanded from somewhere up ahead. *Who is that?* A pair of men stood behind Steve in the doorway, handguns trained on him. The taller of the two men wore jeans, a brown coat, and a wide-brimmed hat. The shorter one donned a clean deputy uniform, his hair cut short. Ryan couldn't make out many more of their features because of how dark it was, though.

Steve went rigid. He closed his eyes and sighed. When he opened them again, he smiled at Ryan. "Well, how about that? Must be your *second* lucky day." He raised his arms and released the hammer on his colt.

The officers moved in to detain him. The one with the hat snatched Steve's firearm and forced the man's hands behind his back. There was a sound like the jingling of chains, and then handcuffs clicked around Steve's wrists.

As he was arrested, Steve's focus remained on Ryan. "Third time's the charm," he hissed. "You brats won't get so lucky next time."

The officer with the hat handed Steve off to the deputy next to him. "Shut up," he said to Steve, then looked at the deputy. "Read him his rights, take him back to the station, and clean him up. We're gonna have a nice long chat, just me and him."

"Oooh, kinky," Steve muttered. He whistled before being shoved out of the room.

Ryan's legs suddenly gave out from beneath him, but Chyann and Willy caught him before he could hit the floor. His head throbbed, and he was sure he had a concussion at least.

His friends lowered him into a sitting position, then sank to the floor next to him and wrapped him up in a tight embrace. Although his whole body ached, he wasn't going to let that stop him from hugging them back.

"You kids okay?" Ryan glanced up and realized the man standing over them was Sheriff Greyson. Stubble covered the sheriff's jawline, messy black hair sticking out from under his hat. The last time Ryan remembered seeing the sheriff was over a year ago when the man had stopped by the house to talk to Grandpa Magnus.

"More or less," Ryan replied.

Sheriff Greyson offered a hand. "Let's get you three outta here." His eyes darted up for a second, his lips parting in shock, and Ryan knew he must have seen the body of the witch hanging behind them.

Ryan took the sheriff's hand and allowed the man to help him to his feet. Chyann and Willy supported him from either side, and together they trudged out of the room, the sheriff following close behind.

They started up the steps leading out of the basement, and Ryan cast a final glance at the hollow-eyed corpse. She disappeared from sight as Sheriff Greyson pulled the double doors closed.

EPILOGUE

ALCOHOL BURNED RYAN'S FACIAL wounds as his mother pressed a cotton pad against his swollen cheeks. He winced at every touch, no matter how light or heavy. He sat on his bed, his mother next to him while she worked.

"And you three have zero idea why this guy wanted to hurt you?" Sheriff Greyson asked, standing in the doorway of Ryan's bedroom. Chyann and Willy–who both stood around the bed–shook their heads.

"No idea," Ryan answered. "We barely got away from him the first time."

The sheriff tilted his head. "Back at the construction site, right?"

Ryan winced from another burn. "Yeah. We managed to sneak away from him. Not sure how the building came down after that, though." He glanced between the sheriff and his mom. "We didn't say anything before because we heard he got hurt, and we figured no harm, no foul."

"Still 'figuring' that after today?" his mom asked with a huff.

Ryan sighed. The "relieved he was okay" phase seemed to be over, and it appeared the "angry because he did something dumb" stage was up next. "Definitely not," he mumbled.

Sheriff Greyson cracked a smile, scratched his cheek, and turned away to leave. "Think I've got everything I need for now. I'll tell the uniforms to clear out and give you guys some space." He headed down the hall.

Ryan's mom watched the sheriff go, then pressed the cotton pad against Ryan's cheek a few more times and set it aside. "Let that sit for a minute. We'll get fresh bandages on you when I come back." She rose to her feet and followed the sheriff out of the room.

Ryan turned to his friends. "Is it bad?"

Willy shrugged and crossed his arms. "If Sadie is into bloated pumpkins, I think you'll be fine."

Ryan laughed, wincing as he did so. *Man, I can't even smile without every muscle in my face hurting*, he thought.

Chyann slapped Willy's arm. "It looks bad now, but like your mom said, the swelling will go down and you'll look a lot more normal soon."

He nodded and tenderly ran his fingers over his face. Maybe Willy was right about the bloated-pumpkin thing…

"Besides," Chyann continued, sitting next to Ryan, "it could have been a lot worse. If we hadn't found out where Steve was holding you, then…"

"Boss and I would be dead," Ryan finished for her.

She went silent. Held her hands up to her chest. Her gaze fell.

Ryan sighed. He knew this would come back around eventually. "Chy, look, I need to apologize. I shouldn't have tried to force you–"

"I wanna help," she blurted out.

Ryan paused for a moment to process what she'd said. "You… *want* to help now?"

"I do," she replied. "I've been running away from a lot of things lately. I was too scared to deal with what's been happening, and we almost lost you and Boss because of that." She faced Willy. "It's about time I stopped running away and started standing my ground." Willy nodded and smiled at her.

There was a flash in front of Ryan's face, and Boss appeared. "You three now know better than most how dangerous a task protecting Twilight Peak will be."

Willy gave Boss a dismissive wave. "We'll be fine. We took down Helsing, a living doll, and an angry ghost. So, we're actually up four against evil if you count the two times we've whooped Steve."

Boss furrowed his brow. "I seem to recall *you* being the one getting 'whooped.'"

"Did you have your eye closed during those fights, Whiskers?"

"My point being," Boss went on, his tone stern, "you three are inexperienced. Helsing was correct about one thing: our luck will not last forever."

Ryan shrugged. "Then we'll just have to get better at this as we go. We're not much, but I'm pretty sure we're all this town's got. We've gotta step up and play defense."

There wasn't another word spoken on the matter, but as Ryan looked from Boss to Willy to Chyann, he felt empowered. Unimaginable horrors tormented the world, and all of them could be on their way here.

As far as Ryan knew, the safety of Twilight Peak rested solely on his and his friends' shoulders. But that didn't worry him now. Because now, the four of them were a united front in the ongoing war against evil.

I'M SURPRISED YOU'RE still here," Grey heard Paige say from behind him. He had paused in the driveway to admire the fiery sky. Twilight Peak always had beautiful sunsets.

He lowered his head but didn't turn around. "I'm surprised you let me stay this long." When she didn't respond right away, he looked back at her.

Paige Myers had always been a pretty woman–at least Grey thought so, ever since he'd met her in high school–with round blue eyes and straight, shoulder-length blonde hair. She was on the petite side, about a half foot shorter than him. She appeared as kind and gentle as ever, but he knew years of pain had hardened her.

They stood for several moments, their eyes locked on one another's, before Paige spoke. "When you bring my son home in one piece, I start feeling a little generous."

Grey grinned. "Sure beats comin' over to chew out Papa Magnus."

Paige's lips turned up in a hesitant smile. "Thank you." Her voice trembled, but it was full of sincerity.

Must've been hard for her to say that to me of all people, Grey thought, and tipped his hat. "Anytime." He continued down the driveway and walked around to the driver's side of his truck.

Pausing with a hand on the door, he watched Paige disappear into her house. Once she was gone, he opened the door and climbed in.

He pulled the door shut, but before he could start the engine, his cell phone buzzed in his pocket. He retrieved the device, swiped the screen, and raised it to his ear. "Yeah?"

"Suspect is booked and waiting for you in interrogation," Griff said on the other end.

"Good. I'll be on my way shortly. Also, can you have Doris get me a full copy of the Hutton casefile?"

"Sure. Mind if I ask what for?"

Grey's gaze traveled over to his passenger seat. "I made a promise." He noticed a folded paper that lay neatly on the seat.

"Uhh, all right." Griff sounded confused. "Fill me in when you get here?"

"Sure thing. See you soon." Grey ended the call, set his phone down, and picked up the folded paper.

His chest tightened when he flipped it over.

The paper was stamped with the same eye-and-triangle symbol he had seen at Ronson's house earlier today. He quickly scanned his surroundings. Who put this here? He hadn't seen it when he'd last been in his truck, and his doors and windows had been locked since he'd left Ronson's place.

Racking his brain for an explanation regarding the paper's sudden appearance, he unfolded it and read the handwritten note it held.

TREAD CAREFULLY, SHERIFF. YOU'RE SWIMMING INTO DANGEROUS WATERS.

Grey lowered the inscription and stared off at the Witch's Woods in front of the Myers house. *What the hell have I gotten myself into?*

LATER THAT NIGHT...

*T*YLER SMOCK HIKED through the trees beneath the fading sunlight. As his boots *crunch*ed against gravel and dirt, he retrieved his camcorder and booted it up.

He flipped open the side, turned the camera toward himself, and waved. "Hey, guys! Ty here. I said I had something special to explore for you once I hit five hundred subs. Tonight, we're gonna check out that place." He paused the recording and continued up the path.

Urban exploration was Tyler's passion. He'd started a YouTube channel a year or so ago to share his interest with others, and thankfully Twilight Peak had a rich history and was full of abandoned buildings. Most people here didn't seem to have the same interests as Tyler did, but that didn't stop him from recording and sharing his hometown with the world.

Tyler readjusted his cap and swept his shaggy white hair away from his glasses. Sunlight had never been easy on him due to his albinism, which was why he did most of his explorations in the evening. That didn't bother him, though. It made for a more exciting time for him, and for a more entertaining video for his subscribers.

Several paces later, Tyler used his free hand to flick on his flashlight, then continued recording. He aimed the camera up at the building looming over him. "Here it is, guys. Say hello to the old Worthrow house." As he glided the device back and forth to get the entire place in the shot, he noticed something new. "What the heck?"

He jogged over to the front gate to get a closer look. Yellow tape with bold black lettering that said *DO NOT CROSS* barred the entrance to the grounds, and the glow coming from Tyler's flashlight glared brightly off the new padlock and set of chains holding the fence shut. *That's weird*, he thought. *These weren't here a few days ago when I came to check the place out.*

Inspecting the top of the fence, he determined that making the climb would be awkward, but he could do it. "Looks like we're goin' over," he said for the camera. "See you guys in a second." He paused the recording and strapped the device to his torso, then set the flashlight on the ground next to the gate so he could easily grab it through the bars on the other side.

It took a few minutes, but he managed to make it over the fence without impaling himself on the spiked bars. After retrieving the rest of his things and resuming his recording, he marched up to the entrance. "Some of you might not know, but this place has a dark history. Most of the sites I cover are abandoned for boring reasons–money, safety, all that kind of stuff." He ran a hand over the cracked wood of the front door. "This place is way different, though."

He pushed the door open and stepped inside. "Long story short, a woman named Samantha Worthrow lived here, and she killed a bunch of kids. She hung herself before the authorities could catch her. They found her in the basement alongside the sewn-up bodies of the kids she took."

Tyler shut the door behind him but left it slightly ajar. "Tonight, I'm gonna go through the place from top to bottom, and I'm gonna see what–"

A loud *thump* echoed from somewhere under the wooden floor. Tyler flinched and directed his camera downward. *What was that?*

He took a deep breath. "It's, uhh…" He stumbled sideways, looking around until he spotted an open doorway to the left. "It's an old house. They make noises sometimes. We've heard stuff like that before. Right, guys?"

He stared at the door. Saw a staircase on the other side. It led down into the dark.

Tyler shrugged and headed for the stairs. "Maybe this time we'll go from bottom to top."

As he descended the steps, they creaked and groaned under his weight, and when he reached the bottom, he shined his flashlight into the room. It was so musty down here he could taste it, and a strange, rotten smell assaulted his nostrils. A broken chair rested against the wall, while a smeared circle of rust... No, that wasn't rust. It was something else. Blood, maybe? "What a mess," he mumbled, directing his flashlight to the right. Just as it shone on another doorway, it died.

Darkness enveloped him, his only illumination that of his camera screen. He fumbled around a bit, shaking his flashlight until the tool flickered back on weakly. The glow it provided was nothing compared to before, but now he could somewhat see, at least.

Before him beckoned a pair of large double doors. He crept over to them, careful not to disturb any of the debris on the floor. Once he reached them, he pushed them open and strode into the next room. Unfortunately, his flashlight didn't extend very far in here, its beams swallowed by the pitch-black.

"Man, this room must be huge, huh? I can't even see all of it." Something like wind whistled behind him, and the double doors slammed shut. At the same time, his flashlight blinked on and off, then went out entirely. "Oh, come on. I just changed these batteries."

He tapped the device against his arm, but the light refused to return. As he desperately tried to revive his tool, his heart beat faster and faster in his chest, beads of sweat forming at his temples. Something told him that he needed to get out of here–that this was wrong, that *this place* was wrong. He wasn't sure how much longer he could put on a casual front for the camera.

What felt like forever passed, and Tyler's flashlight still wouldn't turn back on. He sighed and spun around. "Screw this!" Maybe it would be easier to return in the daytime. He would just have to use sunscreen and–

An odd noise echoed from behind him, and he stopped dead. Was there someone else–some*thing* else–in here with him?

He held his breath and listened. It was difficult to pinpoint exactly what he was hearing. It sounded... wet. Like the slurping noise his dog made when drinking from a water bowl.

Tyler tiptoed around, toward the direction of the sound. He lifted the camcorder and turned on the night-vision function.

His heart almost stopped when he saw what hovered ahead of him.

A woman's corpse hung by a noose that was suspended from a rafter overhead. If Tyler had to guess, he'd say that she was the witch, that the stories about the old sheriff of Twilight Peak leaving her body to decay in the basement were true. He whimpered, still trying to stay as quiet as he could as he looked through the camera screen.

He tilted the device downward to see some rope dangling from one of the corpse's feet onto the floor. As he focused on the ground, he noticed something had been splattered beneath her body. *Is that blood? Wasn't stuff like that in the last room, too? What the hell?*

The rope dangling from the witch's foot wriggled, and Tyler couldn't stifle his gasp as he turned the camera back up to her. He stood frozen as the slurping sound continued. He had to run, had to get out of this awful place, but his legs wouldn't move. He couldn't stop staring at the body, couldn't stop fixating on whatever that noise was.

The rope squirmed again, and Tyler zoomed in on it. With a twinge of fear, he realized it wasn't a rope.

It looked like some sort of tube. A straw made of flesh. It pulsed and twitched as though vacuuming up a dirty floor. Was it sucking up… blood?

He still didn't know what he was looking at, but he'd seen enough. The spell keeping him locked in place broke. He could move again, and it was time to leave.

He pivoted toward the door and pulled on the doorknob, but it wouldn't budge. He pulled again in case it was jammed, but it still wouldn't give. In a frenzy, he pushed the knob. Tugged the knob. Twisted the knob. And then he heard it.

Another noise. This one more of a whisper, a hiss. Like someone breathing onto glass.

He shuddered. A chill blanketed the room, and a loud *crack* echoed all around him. He pivoted. Lifted the camera.

The witch's corpse swayed back and forth. The whispering continued. Another *crack*, and he realized her head was turning to look at him.

Tyler stumbled backward and hit one of the doors. He hadn't seen that, no. It wasn't real. Couldn't be. It was just a dead body, which was scary of course, but it couldn't move.

Except it *had* moved. Was moving. Another *crack* and she was staring down at him with empty black pits. The whispering rose in volume. Erupted into a bloodcurdling scream.

Tyler screamed as well, sliding to the floor.

Through his camera, he watched in horror as the corpse swung toward him.

The rope around her neck snapped, and the last thing Tyler knew was burning, blinding pain.

MALEVOLENCE

Written by:
D.R. Mills

TO BE CONTINUED IN BOOK 5
BLACK

*If you would like to follow D. R. Mills's journey or the **MONSTERS** series specifically, check out the author's official Twitter and Instagram accounts:*

- Instagram: @monsters_bookseries
- Twitter: @MonstersSeries
- Facebook: @Monsters/100067554032850
- TikTok: www.tiktok.com/@monstersseries

If you enjoyed the story, dont forget to leave a review on your preferred platform! Reviews help authors find more readers, and if you'd like D. R. Mills to be able to release books faster, reviews are the best way to support him.

READ THE PREQUEL

ACKNOWLEDGEMENTS

Here we are again. Feels like it's been a minute, huh? I hope by now you've read *Fated Encounters*. I'm very happy with how that one turned out, and it'll give you some information that will be important down the line. But enough about *that* book. Let's talk about *this* book.

This year has been really rough for me to say the least. Things went way off course, big changes had to be made, and I really struggled with a couple of the books I'm working on. It's a good thing I'm stubborn. It feels a bit somber, but I'm also really glad that this book is the one I'm capping off 2023 with. It's kind of fitting in a weird way that only my brain understands. Maybe it's because it's the start of a new beginning.

Up until this point, the main four have been struggling to get on the same page, and by the end of this book, they finally get there.

Maybe it's a sign that next year is going to be the same for me. That being said, there is now a newsletter you can follow for updates and teasers. (And ramblings.) I'm sure it was linked in here already somewhere, but if you missed it, you can always check the social platforms for it, or check the Sea of Ink website for it. Emails go out on the 19th of every month. (It's very cool and you should check it out.)

Books don't make it this far without an author, and authors DEFINITELY don't make it this far without lots and lots of support, so here's a shout out to a few of the people who keep this book train moving forward:

My wife! Emily! She listens to all my incoherent ramblings, and she's always gung ho to drop ideas on me when I'm struggling to think of anything. She's an endless well of support and ideas, and I can't thank her enough.

My editor! Ali! She puts a nice shine on these books so that you guys aren't reading the garbage it started out as. If not for her, this probably wouldn't even BE a book series, so if you like what you're reading, be sure to tell her thank you. She's incredibly talented, and she deserves it. (Also, her books are just as awesome as mine, so I highly recommend checking out her stuff as well.)

My mom! Mom! Can you believe she's still selling more of my own books than I am? Except now there's other stores that have picked up copies of the series as well - all of which sell more books than I do. There's competition breaking out. It's been nonstop love and support since before the books were even books, and I can't thank her enough for not only being such a great mom, but also for being one of my biggest cheerleaders.

My formatters! Enchanted Ink! I can't understand how I'm constantly so blown away with everything they do for me. I always think I won't be surprised by the concepts or designs that the talented Greg Rupel gives back - and time and time again I am wrong. The work Enchanted Ink does is integral to the visual identity of these books, and I can't imagine anybody else doing them justice.

My cover artists! MiblArt! I don't personally know the artists that do my covers, but they're all hired under the company. I am probably the biggest pain in the ass, but they are very patient and professional down to the last email, and the art itself really speaks to their skills. I absolutely love every single cover they've done for me, and I'm glad they're in my corner to make my crazy ideas full-fledged designs.

My readers! You guys! I'm glad everybody is enjoying my weird little stories about these weird little characters and their weird little problems. (Looking at YOU, Steve.) When I was little, I never imagined that one day I would be an author, but I'm glad I am. You guys make the journey worth it, and I hope you enjoy what's coming next.

Finally, a special thanks to my grandma. She's not around to be able to see this book. (Maybe that's a good thing, considering the content.) I know she was damn proud of me, though. We'll cross paths again someday, I'm sure. Thanks for all the books you read to me as a kid. Especially the ones I asked you to read over and over and over...

These sections are weird. I never know what to write to cap things off in a nice way. I was told it would be easier to just copy paste the same thing, but I don't like doing that. I like making these personal little letters to you guys, and to the people who deserve the shout-outs.

At least I can sleep easy knowing that I stuck by my goal despite this crappy year; I had three books hit shelves before the end of it, and there's plenty more on the way. As of right now, I'm in between books twelve and thirteen. Crazy, huh?

Here's to another three (or four) books in 2024.
Until next time.
-DRM

D. R. MILLS

is a young-adult horror author who is currently hard at work on his debut series, *MONSTERS*. He was born and raised in Wyoming, where he's still lurking around somewhere. When he isn't writing, he's playing video games a borderline unhealthy amount or spending time with his beautiful wife.

WWW.SEAOFINKPRESS.WORDPRESS.COM